Cradling her head, he tugged her toward him, covering her mouth with his

Her hands on his chest tensed as if she was ready to push him away. He would have let her go in a heartbeat, but then her fingers relaxed, curled against the knit of his T-shirt.

He wanted to dive inside her mouth, wanted to touch her everywhere. He drew the tip of his tongue across the seam of her lips, the taste of her driving him wild. She didn't pull away, but she didn't immediately open to him, either, and it was obvious she wasn't too sure she wanted things going any further.

He thought his heart would pound out of his chest, but he started to back away. She grabbed his T-shirt, keeping him right there. "Just a kiss," she gasped out. "Just one."

There wasn't any way in hell he could deny her.

Dear Reader,

So—it's the new year. Time for new beginnings. And we at Special Edition take that very seriously, so this month we offer the first of six books in our new FAMILY BUSINESS continuity. In it, a family shattered by tragedy finds a way to rebuild. *USA TODAY* bestselling author Susan Mallery opens the series with *Prodigal Son,* in which the son who thought he'd rid himself of the family business is called back to save it—with the help of his old (figuratively speaking) and beautiful business school nemesis. Don't miss it!

It's time for new beginnings for reader favorite Patricia Kay also, who this month opens CALLIE'S CORNER CAFÉ, a three-book miniseries centered around a small-town restaurant that serves as home base for a group of female friends. January's kickoff book in the series is *A Perfect Life,* which features a woman who thought she had the whole life-plan thing down pat—until fate told her otherwise. Talk about reinventing yourself! Next up, Judy Duarte tells the story of a marriage-phobic man, his much-married mother…and the wedding planner who gets involved with them both, in *His Mother's Wedding.* Jessica Bird continues THE MOOREHOUSE LEGACY with *His Comfort and Joy.* For years, sweet, small-town Joy Moorehouse has fantasized about arrogant, big-city Grayson Bennett…. Are those fantasies about to become reality? In *The Three-Way Miracle* by Karen Sandler, three people—a woman, a man and a child—greatly in need of healing, find all they need in each other. And in Kate Welsh's *The Doctor's Secret Child,* what starts out as a custody battle for a little boy turns into a love story. You won't be able to put it down.…

Enjoy them all—and don't forget next month! It's February, and you know what that means.…

Here's to new beginnings.…

Gail Chasan
Senior Editor

Please address questions and book requests to:
Silhouette Reader Service
U.S.: 3010 Walden Ave., P.O. Box 1325, Buffalo, NY 14269
Canadian: P.O. Box 609, Fort Erie, Ont. L2A 5X3

THE THREE-WAY MIRACLE

KAREN SANDLER

SPECIAL EDITION®

Published by Silhouette Books

America's Publisher of Contemporary Romance

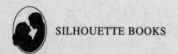 SILHOUETTE BOOKS

ISBN 0-373-24733-8

THE THREE-WAY MIRACLE

Copyright © 2006 by Karen Sandler

Visit Silhouette Books at www.eHarlequin.com

Printed in U.S.A.

Books by Karen Sandler

Silhouette Special Edition

The Boss's Baby Bargain #1488
Counting on a Cowboy #1572
A Father's Sacrifice #1636
His Baby To Love #1686
The Three-Way Miracle #1733

KAREN SANDLER

first caught the writing bug at age nine when, as a horse-crazy fourth grader, she wrote a poem about a pony named Tony. Many years of hard work later, she sold her first book (and she got that pony—although his name is Ben). She enjoys writing novels, short stories and screenplays and has produced two short films. She lives in Northern California with her husband of twenty-three years and two sons who are busy eating her out of house and home. You can reach Karen at karen@karensandler.net.

To Dudley and Sable, who taught countless kids to ride with careful patience and good humor. May the grass always be tall and sweet and the carrots never ending.

Prologue

"Ashley, wake up," Sara Rand whispered to her twelve-year-old sister.

Grabbing Ashley's slender shoulder, Sara gave it a shake, then covered her sister's mouth with her hand when she sat up, yelping with surprise. Even in the bedroom's dim light, Sara could see the dark bruise on Ashley's cheek.

"Daddy's passed out," Sara said softly, "but I don't know for how long."

Sara had already thrown T-shirts, jeans and underwear in their father's old duffel bag and had dragged it out to the wreck of a car in the driveway. She and Ashley didn't have much—most of their meager wardrobe was thrift store castoffs—but it was enough to give them a start.

Thankfully their drunken excuse for a father hadn't found the envelope Sara had hidden under the mattress or they wouldn't have had even that small sum of cash to help them in their escape. At sixteen, she'd been working nearly three years, but rarely kept the money she made.

Sara dropped the T-shirt and jeans on the bed and shifted anxiously from foot to foot as Ashley dressed. She held her breath, listening for the slightest sound from the living room where her father had sprawled on the sofa after polishing off a pint of gin. Once he went down for the count, he rarely woke until morning, but there was that rare occasion when he roused during the night, shouting and stomping down the hall, demanding that Sara get up and make him something to eat.

Sara hustled Ashley through the living room past their snoring father. When Ashley kicked over an empty beer bottle, sending it clattering across the floor, Sara thought her heart would stop. But Hank Rand didn't stir. They slipped from the house without incident and made it to the ancient sedan, Sara in the driver's seat, Ashley beside her.

Sara had just released the parking brake to let the car roll silently from the driveway before starting it, when Ashley grabbed her arm. "Mama's picture! I forgot it!"

Foot still on the brake, Sara shook her head. "We'll have to leave it behind."

Tears filled Ashley's eyes, then trickled down the ugly bruise on her face. "Sara, please. I hid it on the closet shelf."

How could she possibly say no? Sara yanked on the parking brake and shoved open the car door again. Running across the lawn, she slowed to tiptoe up the wooden porch steps. When she opened the front door, her father still snored on the sofa.

As quickly as she could, she hurried to the bedroom she'd shared with her sister for nine years. It took her a few moments to find the photo; her sister had shoved it in the back corner of the closet shelf to keep it from their father's view. The photo had been folded in half, a crease running across their mother's chin, but the image was still dear to Ashley.

She'd nearly made it to the front door when her father woke. "What the hell's going on?" he yelled.

She was too terrified to look back at him. Fumbling with the front doorknob, she thought for sure he'd catch her before she could flee. His footsteps thundered in her ears as she wrenched the door open, his curses striking her like blows.

By some miracle, Ashley had gotten the car started and had backed it from the driveway without hitting anything. Shoving open the driver's side door, Ashley scooted over to give Sara the seat. Sara got inside and slammed the door, barely avoiding her father's punishing grasp. Hitting the accelerator, she prayed the car wouldn't stall. She took off, fishtailing down the street.

"Did you get it?" Ashley asked.

Her hand shaking, Sara handed the crumpled photo to her younger sister. Nodding in response to Ashley's fervent thanks, Sara looked reflexively in the rearview mirror. If her father was there, he was lost in the darkness.

Turning toward the freeway, Sara took deep breaths to

calm herself. They were free. They'd left the nightmare behind.

She pulled onto the ramp heading west. Sara and her sister headed toward a new life.

Chapter One

Sara Rand waved goodbye to her next-to-last student as the boy climbed into his mother's minivan. Jeremy offered a rakish grin in return before the door slid shut, then the minivan retreated down the gravel driveway of the Rescued Hearts Riding School. The car turned right onto Stony Creek Road toward the tiny Sierra Nevada foothill town of Hart Valley. Jeremy's mother had promised him a bowl of ice cream at Nina's Café.

Only Grace Thorne remained, the last of Sara's charges in this week's summer horse camp session. Grace's mother had dropped her off that morning, dashing in from her well-worn sedan, turning Grace over to Sara's teenage assistant, Dani, then hightailing it out again. She'd left in such a hurry Sara hadn't had a chance to talk to her or even meet her. Sara knew only what the little girl's therapist had been able to tell her—that Grace's father had died a year ago and Grace had not spoken a word since.

She'd hoped to have all the children picked up before Keith Delacroix arrived. The Rescued Hearts program director, Jameson O'Connell, had arranged for Delacroix Construction to volunteer a few man-hours to fence the pasture into paddocks. Sara would need some time to show Keith around and give him a rundown on how she wanted the pasture divided. She hated to ask Dani to stay behind to keep an eye on Grace. But her only alternative was to let the little girl tag along as she gave Keith his tour.

She suspected the builder might object to Grace's presence. She didn't know him except by reputation. Although she often saw the Delacroix Construction trucks around town, she'd only crossed paths once with Keith himself in Nina's Café.

The tall, broad-shouldered man with dark blond hair and a serious expression on his face had finished his meal just as she sat down. His gaze had passed over her as he took his check to the register, then he'd glanced back at her as he took his change. Her stomach had clenched at the lack of emotion in those piercing blue eyes. Not coldness, but emptiness.

It might be her own history that made her so wary of Keith Delacroix. But she'd just as soon have Grace gone before he arrived.

The eight-year-old perched on a wooden bench beside the covered riding arena, hands folded in her lap, fair blond head tipped up as she stared out into the trees beyond the pasture. She didn't squirm with impatience; there was not an ounce of fidget in Grace's small feet. She sat perfectly still, perfectly quiet.

Like many kids whose world had careened out of control, where everything they'd trusted had been torn away, Grace held tightly onto the only thing she could—her own behavior. She'd completed every task asked of her today without the least complaint. Halter the horse, lead the horse, tie the horse and brush it. Clean its feet, bring out the saddle and bridle. She did it all. Sara had never seen a more compliant eight-year-old.

Except when Sara asked her to share her name with the other children in the camp group. No amount of prodding could induce Grace to make a sound. The little girl hadn't spoken once in the entire six hours she'd been here today.

The sound of a car engine caught Sara's attention, and she tensed in expectation of seeing one of the white Delacroix Construction trucks approach. She'd learned to feel comfortable around men after years of conscious effort. She'd even managed to forge friendships with a few. But she couldn't seem to squelch the fear, however faint, when she first met someone new. Her brief encounter with Keith in the café only seemed to make the anticipation worse.

A rattletrap muscle car packed with teens came into view on Stony Creek Road, its engine roaring. The driver gunned the engine as the wreck sailed by the NJN Ranch—named for Nate, Jameson and Nina O'Connell—and disappeared toward town. The sudden jolt of sound sent her heart rate up, adding to her anxiety.

The late spring heat and the weight of her auburn hair on her neck added to her discomfort. Sweat melted the thick ponytail against her back where her tank top dipped low. She lifted the hair from her neck and let the faint breeze cool her skin.

Sara had insisted Grace wait in the shade and now she turned to the towhead with a smile. "Your mother should be here soon."

Grace's gaze flicked in Sara's direction, the faintest trace of rebellion in the little girl's blue eyes, before she resumed studying the tall pines beyond the pasture. Rebellion—because she didn't want to see her mother? Or because she didn't want to leave?

Sara checked her watch. Nearly three-thirty. Keith was due any minute. She supposed she'd better take Grace over to Dani so she could give the builder her full attention.

She held a hand out to Grace. "Let's go see what Dani's doing, sweetheart."

Grace scooted off the bench and they started toward the pasture where her teenage assistant was coaxing a dose of bute into old Dudley. Dani had mixed the bitter-tasting anti-inflammatory with some sweet feed, hoping to get enough of the medication into the twenty-five-year-old gelding to ease his arthritis.

"Can you watch her a few minutes, Dani? Just until her mother gets here?"

Dani smiled. "Come on in, short stuff."

Sara unhooked the gate to let Grace through, then headed back toward the arena. She might as well get the tack organized while she waited.

She'd just gathered up a halter and bridle left behind by the campers when she heard the sound of tires on gravel. There was no mistaking the big white pickup truck turning into the driveway. The sun's glare on the windshield obscured the driver's face, but she could see his well-muscled arm resting on the open window.

Keith drove slowly along the driveway, minimizing the dust kicked up by his truck. The dust did the horses no good, especially the somewhat elderly geldings and mares she used for the camp program. Somehow that small kindness eased the knot inside Sara.

The truck angled toward the parking area at the far end of the arena and pulled in next to Dani's little red car. A bit too close—he could only open his truck door halfway. Sara remembered those broad shoulders, the tall frame. There was no way he'd be able to squeeze his way out of his truck unless he moved it.

The door shut again and she saw him slide across the bench seat. When he stepped out of the cab, the midafternoon sun marked his face with shadows. The distance between them gave Sara only the impression of his size, the stiff set of his shoulders, the length of his legs.

She couldn't hold back a habitual stab of fear. She'd become adept at acknowledging it, then setting it aside. As he drew close enough that she could make out the rugged lines of his face and his sharp blue eyes, her fear faded, washed away by a sense of awareness that shocked her.

"Sara Rand? Keith Delacroix." He put out his hand as he approached.

The impulse to protect herself pushed words from her mouth. "I don't think we can do this today."

He dropped his hand, slowing as he continued toward her. When he stopped maybe a couple yards away, he towered over her, seeming a foot taller than her five-seven.

He frowned down at her. If anything, he looked even grimmer than the day at the café, and full of tension. "I canceled an appointment to be here today."

Now that he was closer, fear flickered to life again inside her. She thrust it aside. "I'm sorry. One of the students is still here. Her mother's late picking her up."

He directed his gaze toward the pasture. "Can't the girl watch her?"

Of course she could. She'd already arranged it with Dani. "I'll have to excuse myself when Grace's mother arrives."

His jaw tightened; in irritation she supposed. But when he looked off toward the pasture again, he'd relaxed his expression into careful neutrality.

Sara turned to check on Dani and Grace. They'd pulled grooming tools from the caddy by the pasture gate and were brushing Dudley as the old gelding grazed.

When she turned back to Keith, he stared down at her, the intensity of his blue eyes unnerving. "Let's get started." He put his hand on Sara's arm.

The heat of his touch jolted through her and she pulled away with a gasp. She trembled in shock, not because the light press of fingers had frightened her, but because of her sensual awareness of it.

She rubbed her arm, not liking the sensation. "Sorry."

She wasn't even sure what she was apologizing for. "If you'll follow me."

She led him past the small octagonal structure that served as her home and office. He walked alongside her, shortening his stride to keep pace with her. "You teach kids to ride here?"

"I help kids work through their problems." He felt too close and she edged away. "Sometimes on horseback, sometimes on the ground."

They reached the knoll that overlooked the pasture and arena, a good vantage point to explain how she wanted the paddocks laid out. Below them, Grace and Dani fed carrots to the horses.

"The horses represent the problems these kids face." Sara looked out over the gently rolling landscape. "They learn to handle the horses and deal with their frustrations, their fears and their sorrows at the same time."

He paced across the knoll, his work boots scuffing through the dry grass. "Nice spot."

She gestured out at the pasture. "I want six paddocks, each about twenty-five by fifty feet. On that end, where the oak trees will give the horses some shade."

"Easy enough." Propping his boot on a boulder jutting from the knoll, he bent to tighten his laces. His thigh muscles flexed under his jeans as he pushed off and resumed his restless stroll. "Beautiful piece of land. Jameson could have gotten a hell of a lot of money for it if he'd sold it."

"I would have thought he'd keep it. Build a house for him and Nina."

Keith paused to pick up a piece of quartz crystal. "Too many bad memories." He dropped the quartz in the grass.

Sara glanced over at him, wondering if he'd elaborate. She doubted he would. "So Jameson's a friend of yours?"

"Yeah. Worked for me a couple years ago. Damn good carpenter."

That was a surprise. Still fairly new in Hart Valley, Sara knew Jameson was co-owner of the café in town with his wife, Nina. She'd heard whispers that he'd once been in prison and that some of his grandmother's wealth had filtered down to him. Jameson had donated the land, but it was his grandmother, Lydia Heath, whose largesse mainly funded the program.

Down in the pasture, Grace wrapped her small arms around Dudley's neck. The patient old horse stood stock-still. "I'll need to get a barn up before winter. These old horses will need shelter when the rains hit."

He looked over his shoulder at her. "I'm only here to fence the paddocks." His blue eyes seemed to bore into her, digging into the barriers she kept around herself. "I can't build the barn, too."

"I wasn't asking you to."

"It was a royal pain setting aside the time as it is. If I didn't owe Jameson—"

"I appreciate anything you can do."

He looked even more annoyed at her words. "Fencing is easier with a two-man crew, but I can't spare anyone for this."

Did he want her help? In another man, she might have suspected it was a smarmy attempt to get close to her. But his shuttered expression told her he'd rather she wasn't around at all. Certainly he wouldn't ask if the need wasn't genuine.

"I'd be glad to help."

"Do you know a damn thing about fencing?"

"I worked a summer on a dude ranch. I'm not the expert you are, but I know which end of a hammer to hold."

"Fine, then. I'll do what I can on my own—give you a holler if I need a second pair of hands."

"It won't be a problem as long as the kids aren't here. I just want the work done."

He nodded. "What kind of barn?"

"Just pipe panels, metal roof."

His mouth set in a hard straight line. "This week is all I could spare. Just for the paddocks."

"I realize that."

"Jameson should have mentioned the barn."

"I'm sure he didn't want to overburden you."

Dani's laughter snagged Sara's attention and she turned to see her assistant bringing Grace toward her. Keith watched them, as well, his gaze riveted on the pair.

His voice was hoarse when he spoke. "Is that Grace?"

"Yes. Grace Thorne. Her mother should be here any minute."

"My God." He wheeled away, started down the knoll.

She and Dani exchanged puzzled looks, then Sara followed Keith. "Mr. Delacroix—"

He shouted back at her. "I've got to go."

He'd just rounded the end of the arena when a car pulled into the driveway. Grace's mother, here at last.

Keith froze as Alicia Thorne bypassed the parking spaces and stopped over by the arena gate. He stared at Alicia's car as if the devil himself were inside.

Dust still swirling, Alicia stepped from her car and stood thunderstruck. "Keith?"

His hands clenched tight as he faced Grace's mother. "Hello, Alicia."

Why couldn't the past just leave him alone?

Keith had done everything he could to avoid Alicia the past year. The few times he'd seen her in town, having dinner at Nina's Café or up in Marbleville doing her shopping, he'd left as quickly as he could. He'd felt like a complete coward and a total jerk, but he just didn't want to deal with the memories.

And now, watching Grace walk over to her mother and give her a polite hug, the memories returned suddenly. It didn't help that the bubbly little girl he remembered had warped into someone else, someone old and world-weary. The child she'd been a year ago had been sunny and good-natured, confident she was the center of her universe.

He felt Sara Rand's gaze on him, could sense the questions. Damned if he'd answer any of them. She'd rattled him enough already with her determined expression, the auburn hair that wisped around her cheeks where it had escaped her ponytail. The fire in her hazel eyes seemed to shift with the light—now green, now light brown with gold flecks. Why couldn't the woman's eyes settle on a single color?

It didn't matter. He wasn't going there. She was a nice enough woman, but so was Alicia, so were the dozen or so eligible women in Hart Valley. Nice didn't matter to him anymore. He was just managing to hold his life together. A woman, nice or otherwise, might make it fly apart again.

Sara looked at Alicia. "You know each other?"

Alicia stared at Keith. "Everyone knows everyone in Hart Valley," she said softly.

If he didn't get out of here, he'd explode. "Can we finish this later?"

"When?" Sara asked.

He stepped carefully around Alicia. "Tomorrow morning."

What happened next stopped him in his tracks. Grace left her mother's side and lifted her arms to him. The pain inside him sharpened.

"Hi, sweetheart." He knelt and gave her a hug, her small arms barely spanning the breadth of his shoulders. "How are you?"

Of course she didn't answer. That was why she was here, apparently. She was one of Sara's "kids with problems."

As he straightened again, Alicia met his gaze briefly and he saw a glint of tears in her eyes. Then she turned to Sara. "I'm so sorry I'm late." She tipped her chin up. "I'm afraid Grace won't be able to continue with camp."

The little girl, still holding his hand, tensed beside him. He ought to leave. He didn't want to know anything more about Grace's and Alicia's lives. But those small fingers gripping his hand kept him rooted to the spot.

Sara looked up at him, concern in those intriguing eyes. "I really think she'll do well with the program if we could just give it a chance."

Alicia shook her head. "There's no way to get her here every morning or pick her up on time in the afternoon. My boss nearly had a coronary today when I left early."

He really ought to keep out of it, ought to just walk away. "Could she bring her early, pick her up late?"

"I'm sorry." He heard real regret in Sara's tone. "The insurance company is very picky about when the kids are here. Only during program hours."

Beside him, Grace seemed to shrink even more into herself. She let go of his hand and grabbed her mother's, clinging as if the world's weight would snatch her away.

"Maybe in the fall," Alicia said. "The workload might lighten up."

He suspected she only said that to soothe Grace, not because she thought it might be possible. He only had to see the little girl's bowed head to know Grace wasn't buying it.

Without thinking, he jumped on a hand grenade. "Someone else could bring her."

Sara's gaze fixed on him. "Are you volunteering?"

No! He couldn't. There was no way. He couldn't take this path again, risk tearing open those wounds.

He nodded toward the teenage girl now heading for her car. "How about her?"

Sara shook her head. "Dani's only sixteen. She still has a provisional driver's license. She can't transport anyone without an adult present."

Grace looked up at him, hope in her sweet face. He'd be here every day, it made perfect sense to transport her. How could he refuse?

"I'll do it," he said, with a casualness that was a complete lie. "What time?"

Sara studied him and he saw the questions again. "We start at eight-thirty. You can bring her as early as eight. Dani will be here."

"Fine. That's no problem."

"Camp ends at two-forty-five, so we like the children picked up by three."

"Most days I'll be here working, but if I'm not I'll be sure to be back."

It was a miracle he could keep his voice so even, so neutral, even though inside he felt close to meltdown. He'd managed to avoid that kind of catastrophe for months, didn't intend to let go now in front of Sara.

"I should go. Be back in the morning."

Alicia grabbed his hand. "Thank you. Thank you so much."

He pulled away. "You still live in the same place?"

"Yes," Alicia said. "But she'll be at the day care. The Johnston's place—Linda and Wes."

"I'll pick her up there at quarter to eight."

He nodded to Sara and something in her face—approval, compassion—steadied him, quieting the roiling pain inside him. He forced himself to look away, his gaze falling instead on Grace.

The look of gratitude on her delicate face was like a punch to the gut. His throat tightened and he thought he was lost again.

Turning away, he hightailed it to his truck. He had to gulp in air to stop the shaking, had to count to ten before he could safely start the engine. Then through sheer force of will, keeping his mind utterly blank, he pulled slowly down the driveway and out onto Stony Creek Road.

Considering the tension she'd seen in him, Sara half expected Keith to gun his engine and tear down the gravel driveway. But he controlled his speed, only raising the minimum of dust on the bone-dry surface. He didn't accelerate until he reached the paved road at the end of the driveway, turning away from Hart Valley.

Alicia started her car and as she backed away from the arena, Grace turned toward Sara and lifted her hand in the smallest of waves. Sara smiled and waved back, the sweetness of Grace's gesture clutching at her heart.

Sara had once tried to resist the emotions the kids stirred in her, tried to pretend they didn't touch her deeply. But not only had it been impossible, it wasn't necessary. These children, so many of them as broken as she, would never be her enemy.

Keith Delacroix was another matter. She'd never be able to let her guard down with him, not completely. An unfortunate byproduct of his gender, his size. She could be friendly to him—if he opened up even that much—she could work beside him. But the walls would stay up.

So who was he to Alicia and Grace? The little girl hadn't offered a hug to anyone else here, hadn't seemed to have that kind of affection in her. She barely responded that warmly to her own mother. But Keith represented something to her.

Sara didn't know what was the more intriguing puzzle—the silent little girl or the imposing, serious-faced man. Lucky for her, it wasn't her job to figure out Keith Delacroix. That path of discovery might just be treacherous. Better to stay on the familiar ground of a troubled little girl.

Chapter Two

The next morning, Keith drove away from Linda and Wes Johnston's day care center. Grace was seated silently beside him, her pink vinyl backpack clutched in her lap. In his rearview mirror, he saw Linda still on her front walk, wheels turning madly as she speculated on what might be going on between him and Alicia.

Linda might not be an official member of the Hart Valley busybodies, as Jameson O'Connell liked to refer to the gossiping old biddies that gathered at Nina's Café, but the babysitter relished scandal.

She'd waited until Grace had climbed in the truck and out of earshot before she'd started in. "I didn't know you and Alicia were still in touch."

"We're not. Just doing her a favor."

Linda couldn't leave it at that. "Could have knocked me over with a feather when she called last night to tell me you'd be driving Grace to horse camp. How long's it been since—"

"Gotta get to work." There was no way in hell Keith would be having this conversation.

He took another glance in the rearview mirror before he turned at the stop sign. Linda had gone inside, no doubt to tell her husband, Wes, all the little details, real and imagined.

Let her talk. He was immune to gossip; it had been the least of his worries a year ago when the busybodies served him and his troubles up like a banquet. He didn't let it get to him then and he wouldn't now. Better to keep his focus on the present.

But channeling his mind into the here and now brought his thoughts to equally dangerous territory—Sara Rand. Her stubborn expression, the auburn hair that wisped around her cheeks where it had escaped her ponytail, the fire in her intriguing eyes. That he'd noticed her at all, had had any awareness of her as a woman startled him. He'd thought he'd numbed himself so thoroughly that nothing as sweet as Sara Rand could creep under his skin.

Not that he'd let her get any farther. Keith redirected his attention to navigating his way out of the Johnstons' rabbit warren of a housing development. The Sierra Nevada foothills housing boom had arrived in Marbleville County, turning what used to be expansive pasture land into quarter acre parcels with cookie-cutter houses. Delacroix Construction had built several in this development over the past two years.

He'd been reading over the plans for a house the next block over from the Johnstons' the night he got the phone call from Deputy Gabe Walker. He could still remember the bitter taste in his mouth when Gabe told him solemnly about the accident. He'd dropped the phone, the portable skittering across the kitchen floor.

The nastiness that followed became fodder for Hart Valley's active rumor mill for weeks afterward, turning him into a near hermit the few hours he wasn't working. If he'd been a workaholic before Melissa's death, he was a mindless machine afterward, piling as many hours of labor into his life as possible to drown out the heartbreak.

He shook off the memories. "Looking forward to camp today?" Keith asked the slender child beside him.

Several long seconds passed before Grace shrugged. The youngster's silence was downright eerie, especially since he remembered her endless chattering before her father died. It had been difficult for Melissa sometimes when they visited the Thornes, listening to Grace, knowing their own son would have been her age if he'd lived.

Keith put a lid on the emotion that crept up inside him. He rarely let himself think about Christopher, didn't like revisiting the bleakness of when that short life ended. He'd learned it was best to refocus on the present.

And again Sara Rand's pretty face popped up in his consciousness like a prickly sprout of blackberry vine you could never quite eradicate. Blackberries grew everywhere in the foothills, bursting up out of the ground in the most inhospitable places. If you could live with the thorns, the mid-July berries were a taste of heaven.

Like Sara Rand would be if he were crazy enough to let himself get that close. He wouldn't—he had enough thorns piercing his heart.

The moment Keith pulled into the driveway at the ranch, something sparked inside Grace and she squirmed in her seat, the vinyl backpack crinkling as she hugged it to her chest. As he parked his truck beside the red car, the little girl turned as far as she could in her seat belt, her expression eager, her gaze fixed on the arena where the old gelding rolled in the dirt.

He scanned the ranch for someone he could hand Grace over to, but he saw only the teenage girl—Dani?—he'd seen yesterday. She walked along the far side of the arena, leading a fly-specked gray pony and a bay mare, one on each side, toward the tie racks by the tack room.

If Sara was here, she was well-hidden. He'd assumed she lived in the small house on the property, but there wasn't another car in sight. Maybe someone dropped her off, her boyfriend or even her husband. Keith hadn't noticed a ring, but working around horses, she probably left her rings at home.

What did it matter if Sara was involved, married or single? He wasn't the least bit interested. He just needed someone to take care of Grace. He had an appointment that morning, to meet a client at Nina's Café in an hour. He hadn't been able to reschedule after he'd committed to the work here.

After unbuckling her seat belt, Grace rose to her knees and stared out the back window at the pony and mare by the tie rack. It was as if the horses were a talisman that called her from her silent world.

He might as well take Grace over there. He wouldn't feel right leaving her with Dani, not when the teenager had the horses to deal with. But he could wait a few minutes until one of the other helpers showed up.

Or until Sara did.

It really didn't matter if it was the auburn-haired program director or someone else. Any other responsible person would be fine. Then he could leave with a clear conscience.

As he approached, Dani greeted him with a smile. "Hi, Mr. Delacroix. Hey, Grace."

No answer from the eight-year-old. Her face as solemn as ever, she stuffed her backpack into one of the cubbies set up outside the tack room, then stood silently as if waiting for orders.

Keith took another look around. "I hate leaving you here alone with her. I know you're busy."

On tiptoes, Dani grinned at him over the withers of the mare she was grooming. "That's okay. Sara will be right back."

He ignored the rush of excitement inside him. "Great. I wanted to go over the materials list with her."

Which he could do later, after his meeting with his new client. But if they discussed the list beforehand, he could pick up what was needed before he returned. At least that's what he told himself.

The crunch of gravel alerted him to the arrival of a pristine four-by-four pickup, jacked up on massive tires. A man in a power suit stepped from the truck; probably one of the Johnston's well-heeled neighbors. The little boy who bolted from the other side of the pickup ran so fast he sent up clouds of dust and startled the old mare from her doze at the tie rack.

The man in the suit barked an order at his son, stopping the boy in his tracks. Even as the child stood shamefaced, the man continued berating him until Keith was about to give the father a piece of his mind.

"Jeremy, someone misplaced Sable's bridle yesterday. Would you go look for it in the tack room?"

Sara's firm voice cut off the businessman's harangue. She stepped past the horses, with a glance to Dani, then passed within inches of Keith. He caught the faintest whiff of her scent, as if she'd slept in a bed of lavender.

She stood with shoulders back. "Thank you, Mr. Wilkins. We'll see you at three."

"The hell you will," the businessman said in a nasty tone. "The ex is picking up the brat."

With two strides, Keith stood beside Sara. "You keep a civil tongue in your head when you talk to her."

"Who the hell are you?" Wilkins blustered in response.

Keith gripped his hands tight at his sides to keep from giving the businessman a poke. "It doesn't matter. Just watch your mouth."

He gave Keith a dismissive once-over. He wasn't quite as tall as Keith's six foot three, but his shoulders were broad. From gym workouts, no doubt, rather than honest labor.

With a sneer, the man turned on his heel and marched

back to his one-ton truck. A thick cloud of dust billowed up in the pickup's wake. He nearly sideswiped a battered Jeep pulling into the driveway.

Sara turned on Keith, hazel eyes snapping with anger. "I don't appreciate you interfering."

Her ire stung. "I couldn't let him talk to you that way."

"Believe me, I know how to handle rude parents. Rile him up and he'll just take it out on his son."

Shaking the tension from his hands, he dragged in a breath, then regretted it when he caught the fragrance of lavender again. "I didn't mean to intrude. I just…" He couldn't seem to put together the logic of what he'd intended. "Sorry."

He wasn't really. The man had needed more than a verbal dressing down. He'd needed his butt planted in the dirt, that fancy haircut messed up.

Sara's gaze narrowed on him, then she looked over his shoulder. "Ryan, help Grace clean Pearly's feet."

The Jeep's driver, a teen boy with long hair, took Grace's hand and led her to a plastic caddy filled with brushes and hoof picks. A steady stream of cars were arriving now.

Sara returned her focus to Keith. "I have to get to work."

He knew he ought to leave her be and hightail it out of there, but he couldn't let her go yet. "If I could just get a minute."

It didn't look as if she wanted to give him even a second. She shifted her glance to her arriving students, then back to him. "What is it you need?"

As innocent as her question had been, a strand of heat trickled down Sara's spine. When a man looked like him—

wide shoulders straining the knit of his T-shirt, angular face and brilliant blue eyes, close-cropped blond hair begging to be touched—no question seemed innocent.

But she wasn't about to let herself dwell on what she needed. Need had nothing to do with her life. What she wanted, she took action to acquire on her own. Like her job as program director—it had presented some challenges and she knew she couldn't do all of it on her own. So she asked for help as needed, picking and choosing those who worked with her. Lydia Heath, Jameson O'Connell's grandmother and Rescued Hearts main benefactor, had given her that kind of latitude.

But with Keith…she didn't have much choice but to allow him to get closer than she felt comfortable. She'd just have to find a way to deal with the mix of attraction and wariness she felt for him.

Keith nudged her out of the way as Jeremy raced past her with Sable's bridle. "I wanted to talk to you about materials."

He pulled her back as Jeremy dashed across her path again. She didn't like the way his warm touch affected her, sensuality battling with fear.

When one of the children shrieked, taking the noise level up another notch, she used it as an excuse to pull away. "Let's find someplace quieter."

She squeezed past the milling children grooming horses and carrying saddles and bridles. When she glanced back to be certain he followed, Keith seemed to edge through the knot of youngsters as if loath to make contact. He'd been affectionate enough toward Grace yesterday, however brief their hug. But that fondness didn't seem to extend to other children.

He caught up with her as they reached the corner of the covered arena. "We don't have to do this now if they need you back there."

There was that word again. *Need.* Why did it sound like a proposition? "I have a few minutes."

She led him to the pasture, where Dudley wandered in search of any wisps of hay the other horses had missed. With his five equine buddies working today, Dudley's only company was a pair of pygmy goats.

When Dudley wandered over, Keith gave the old gelding's chestnut face an expert rub. What would those hands feel like on her face?

Unbidden, a memory of Victor's hands rose in her mind's eye. The way he'd stroke her cheek tenderly, brush his fingertips across her mouth.

Before he balled them into fists. She clamped the lid on the ugly image.

She and Keith were a good three feet apart, but she stepped back anyway.

He gestured at the wire mesh fencing, slim metal T-posts holding it up and the strand of barbed wire on top. "We'll have to replace all this fence. Not the safest thing for horses."

"What do you suggest?"

He continued his massage of Dudley's forehead, the play of sinews across his hand mesmerizing. "Peeler cores instead of T-posts for starters. Two-inch by four-inch woven horse wire. Stuff with holes this big you risk getting a foot stuck."

A crashing in the thick blackberry vines on the far side of the pasture caught Dudley's attention and the old gelding pulled away from Keith to look. A deer leaped from the clot of vines and dashed across the pasture. Dudley took off in pursuit, head bobbing up each time he stepped on his sore front right foot.

Keith watched him trot a few more steps before the gelding resumed his hay search. "He's lame."

"We're hoping it's a stone bruise, not his arthritis." She sighed. "We were lucky to only have five kids this first camp session or we'd have been short a horse."

Keith swung his head toward her and his gaze fixed on her face. Although he still stood an arm's length away, she felt a wave of heat wash over her. His study of her face seemed as palpable as a touch, tracing along the line of her cheek, the plane of her brow. Then he edged closer and reached toward her.

She should have retreated, should have evaded him. But she stood there, frozen, as he tangled his fingers in her hair a moment, brushed her ear, the corner of her jaw before pulling back.

Turning his hand, he let a bit of oat straw fall to the dusty ground. "You had some hay in your hair." Harshness edged his tone, sending sensation up her spine again.

She could still feel where he'd touched her, as if marked by a silver trail of light.

With an effort, she gathered her thoughts again. "Peeler cores and two-by-four-inch wire." She barely had enough air for the words. "Anything else?"

He stared at her a full five seconds before he answered.

"Hot wire across the top. Instead of the barbwire. To keep them from leaning against it."

A horse would push over a fence to reach a clump of green grass on the other side. "Would electric fencing be safe around the kids?" She had to look at him when she spoke to him, didn't she? Just because the view was so enticing didn't give her permission to be rude.

"It's low voltage. Just enough to warn the horses off the fence."

Low voltage. Unlike her response to those sharp blue eyes. "I'd better get back to the kids." She started toward the arena.

He dogged her steps, close enough she could have brushed her bare arm against his. "I'll just pick up the fencing material for now."

She unhooked the latch on the nearest arena gate. He reached around her to open it for her. She slipped past him into the cool shade of the arena.

He shut the gate, latched it. Then he stood there, staring down at her.

She had to pull away. Her students waited in the arena, clustered around the mounting block, eager to climb on their horses.

His long fingers were still wrapped around the gate. She stretched her hand toward him, didn't quite touch. "Thank you."

"I have to go." He didn't move.

She tipped her head toward the group of horses and impatient children. "And I have a class to teach."

He drew his gaze over her, head to toe. She didn't know

what he was looking for, but his examination left her breathless in its wake.

He nodded brusquely. "Later, then."

With that, he turned on his heel and strode toward his truck. Sara hurried over to the group of horses and riders around the mounting block and started the day's first lesson.

At two-fifteen, Keith pulled his flatbed truck through the large wrought-iron arch spelling out NJN Ranch and onto the gravel driveway. A quick glance in the rearview mirror told him the mini excavator he'd borrowed from a buddy was still secure on the truck's bed. He and Wade had traded equipment and services for years, Keith building a stem wall for Wade's workshop, Wade loaning Keith the Bobcat excavator when he needed it.

Since Sara was still working with the kids in the arena, he eased the flatbed into the spot farthest away. Climbing from the truck, Keith headed over to watch the tail end of the lesson.

Sara stood in the center of the arena, a liver chestnut gelding beside her, Grace in the saddle. The other four students rode in pairs around the arena, each rider holding the end of a ribbon as their horse walked along.

"Okay, everyone trot," Sara called out. "See if you can hang on to your ribbon."

The flea-bitten gray pony trotted past with the bay quarter pony mare beside it. Jeremy, on the gray mare, laughed uproariously as he bounced along, almost immediately losing his end of the ribbon.

"Come on in, Jeremy, Grace will…" Sara spotted Keith and faltered. Despite the thirty feet between them, the impact of her gaze on him was as powerful as if she stood within arm's reach. She turned to Grace. "Go take Jeremy's place."

With the help of the long-haired teen boy, Grace's horse walked out to the rail where the girl on the bay quarter pony waited. As they continued the exercise with the ribbon, Sara crossed the arena toward Keith.

She kept one eye on her students. "I didn't think you'd be so long."

"Sorry. I didn't, either." After his hour-long session with his client this morning, he'd had to deal with a series of crises on three of his job sites—trusses not delivered, electrician a no-show, a problem with the concrete pour. It had taken him until now to get back to the ranch and he still hadn't had a chance to pick up the fencing supplies.

"Jeremy, trade places with Marisa!" she called out, then glanced back at him. "I'm pretty busy."

"I just wanted to know when I should unload the Bobcat."

She looked at him curiously a moment before turning back to the arena. "Jeremy, your horse is too close to Grace's."

"The excavator's pretty damn noisy. I don't want to spook the horses."

"The kids will be dismounting soon. You can drive it over then." One of her assistants yelled for her and she took off across the arena.

His mouth went dry watching her. All soft curves in

her red tank top and denim shorts, she just about stopped his heart. He felt like a regular letch watching her hips sway as she moved, even more so when she bent to pick up the ribbon one of the pairs of riders had lost in the arena footing, presenting her perfectly rounded bottom to him.

He forced himself to turn away and continue toward the flatbed. He hadn't so much as entertained a sexual fantasy since Melissa died. He didn't like it, didn't want the images playing out in his head.

He waited by the flatbed, making a concerted effort to keep his gaze away from the arena. The pines and oaks surrounding the ranch made a pretty picture, the turkey vultures crisscrossing the blue sky overhead a passable distraction. If his attention wandered one or two times back to Sara, at least he wasn't leering. Not much anyway.

As the clock ticked around to two forty-five, parents started pulling in to pick up their kids. The tractor was ready to back off the flatbed and he'd double-checked the auger bit linkages were secure. Leaning against the truck, he watched Sara speak with the parents as her assistants led the unsaddled horses back into the arena.

Once the children returned from the pasture and the parents tucked their kids into cars and minivans, Sara headed off toward the small octagonal house while Dani brought Grace over to him.

Dani smiled as she approached. "Sara will be back in a few minutes. She asked if you could wait before you unload the Bobcat."

"Sure." As Dani helped Grace into the flatbed, he kept

his gaze fixed on the eight-sided house. Not that he had nothing better to do but watch for her, but he'd lost enough time today. The sooner Sara showed up, the sooner he could get things moving.

Finally she came around the side of the house and started toward him. The rear view had been appealing enough; Sara's front had its own charms. He had enough sense to keep his eyes off her breasts, but took in her slender shoulders, with their faint tan, and her pale legs, the skin smooth and silky.

He didn't want to react to her, didn't want to feel anything. He clamped tight on the stirring inside him.

She held out a sealed business-size envelope. "This is for Mrs. Thorne."

He hadn't meant to touch her as he took the envelope, knew it was about the stupidest thing he could do. But somehow, he couldn't get a proper grip on the slim white envelope unless his fingers grazed hers, making only the briefest contact.

He might as well have burned her, the way she jerked back. The envelope fluttered to the dirt. He stared down at it a moment, feeling like an idiot.

He bent to pick it up. "Sorry."

She shoved her hands in the pockets of her shorts. "If you could give it to Grace's sitter."

"Let me get the Bobcat off the truck. Then I'll drop off Grace, be right back. I can get the holes dug at least."

"I'll keep the horses in the arena until you're done."

There was an edge to the mundane conversation, her discomfort obvious. Maybe she'd seen the heat inside him from his not-so-innocent looks at her. Maybe it was just the inadvertent touch. Either way, he'd better keep his distance.

The roar of the Bobcat as Keith started it up pounded Sara's ears, adding to the jitter along her nerves his touch had started. Posting herself beside the passenger side of the truck where Grace sat quietly, Sara watched his expert operation of the excavator as he backed it from the rear of the flatbed. The way the muscles of his arms flexed, his single-minded focus on the task of easing the Bobcat down the ramp, fascinated her far more than she felt comfortable with.

Once he had the excavator on the ground, he sat there waiting, the powerful engine filling the air with noise. "Where?" he mouthed, his voice lost in the din.

She turned to Grace and shouted, "Stay right here, sweetie. Okay?" The little girl nodded solemnly.

Rounding the truck, she gestured him toward the back end of the covered arena. There was a wider access to the pasture there than between the arena and tack room. As he turned that way, she walked behind him.

The horses kicked up their heels a bit at the cacophony, but since she used a small tractor to haul their feed out to them, they were more interested in the possibility of an early dinner. They gathered along the arena rail, six heads all in a row, the more dominant ones baring teeth when they felt their personal space encroached upon.

She hurried ahead to open the pasture gate and he expertly maneuvered the Bobcat inside. Once the engine cut out, she sighed with relief at the quiet. Then Keith climbed from the excavator and ambled over to her. A man that big shouldn't move with such grace.

It struck her then—she was alone with him, the only adult left, no one to step between them, no one to protect her. She couldn't help the flare of panic that surged inside her. When he reached for her, she sucked in a breath, flinching back.

His hand hovered near her cheek. "You have a smudge. Can I…?"

"Okay. Sure." Her voice shook, but she held still as he touched her.

He rubbed at her forehead. "Did you bump your head on something?" She could swear his voice lowered an octave as he spoke.

"Probably a horse kiss," she said, her own voice too soft. The warm air felt cool compared to the heat of his touch.

When was he going to drop his hand, pull away? After all, she needed to breathe and couldn't as long as he maintained that gentle pressure against her brow. She knew she could ease her head from the contact, step back to free herself of the connection, but still she stood there.

One of the horses screamed at another, then the whole group took off at a restless trot across the arena. It was enough of a distraction to bring her to her senses. She bent her head aside and he dropped his hand at last.

"Better go," he muttered as he strode away.

She watched him retrace his steps around the covered arena, willing herself to keep her gaze on the center of his back instead of his broad shoulders, his muscular legs. Maybe she could only imagine the line of his legs in those heavy denim jeans, but fantasy could fill in an awful lot of blanks.

Her father had taught her a compelling lesson—men were stronger than women and if a man chose, that strength could hurt. It wasn't until later when she'd met other men, good men, that she understood that being male didn't mean being a monster, that a man could be a friend as much as a woman could. If she was careful, if she gave a man time to either show his ugliness or demonstrate his humanity, she could usually tell which ones could be trusted to be friends.

But as Keith's flatbed truck drove away, temptation receding, at least temporarily, Sara knew it wasn't likely he would ever be a friend. Not because she didn't trust him— though she didn't. Not yet.

Instead she didn't trust herself to see clearly if this man would hurt her. She'd already lived that nightmare with Victor. She wasn't about to put herself through that again.

Chapter Three

Was he coming back? It was nearly five and Sara had started loading flakes of grass hay in the tractor's small skip loader, on top of the senior horse pellets she'd already scooped there. It was still an hour until feeding time, but she liked to get the hay and pellets ready early if she could.

It had been three-fifteen when Keith finally left with Grace, and Sara knew the little girl didn't live more than fifteen or so minutes away. So maybe Keith had changed his mind about doing the work today. Maybe he'd disappeared off the face of the planet, taking with him the lure of his broad shoulders and muscular arms. That he'd left behind the Bobcat was a bonus; she'd always wanted to try operating one.

She smiled at the fanciful notion as she piled the last

flake of hay in the skip loader. A moment later, her ears caught the roar of a diesel engine and she sighed both in resignation and anticipation. The trick here would be to not let him get anywhere near her, either physically or emotionally. He'd dig his holes and go on his way, leaving her to the peace of her small lonely house.

Of course, she'd have to continue to maintain that distance while Keith finished fencing paddocks. Keeping men at arm's length had never been particularly difficult for her—not after living with her father's brutal hands, even more so after Victor. So keeping herself safe from Keith shouldn't be a problem. She wouldn't let it be.

Keith stopped the truck in the middle of the parking area, then climbed from the cab, diesel engine still running. She couldn't quite make out his face from this distance; the feed room backed up to the tack room and she stood barely clear of the edge of it. But she knew he looked for her, could tell by his stillness, only his head moving as he scanned the property.

Squelching the urge to duck back inside the feed room and hide, she stepped clear of the structure and waved. He started toward her as she approached him. Her heart hammered in her ears and it shocked her that she was so glad to see him. That wasn't good.

She made sure she stopped several feet from him. "I thought you might not make it back today."

"A few more fires to put out at the job sites. Then I had to pick up the fencing and peeler cores." He nodded toward the flatbed. "Okay if I pull the truck around to the pasture? Easier if I unload over there."

"Sure. Just take it slow." Several rolls of wire fencing alongside a pile of what looked like eight-foot long logs were tied down on the flatbed. "Let me get my gloves so I can give you a hand."

"I have a pair." He opened the tool box behind the cab and unearthed leather work gloves. He handed them to her. "Hop in. You can ride over with me."

She wanted to say no, didn't want to be in the truck cab with him. But she didn't like being afraid, either. Fear had consumed so much of her life.

So she climbed into the truck, swallowing back her unease as she shut the door. "Did you put the fencing wire and posts on Jameson's account?"

"Just the fencing." He kept his gaze on the narrow path alongside the arena. "I had the posts at my house."

"I'm sure Jameson doesn't expect you to donate both your time and materials."

"Those gloves going to work?" He drove past the pasture gate, then backed the truck close to the Bobcat. "I might have a smaller pair."

Still clutching them in her lap, Sara had forgotten about them. "These are fine." As she tugged them on, it felt oddly intimate putting her hands where his had been.

They met in back of the truck. He grabbed two of the five-inch-diameter poles and tossed them to the ground. Sara took one and dropped it beside his.

They both put their hands on the same peeler core. Sara backed off and waited for him to take it. "I appreciate your time and the donation, but—"

"Did I see bags of cement over by the tack room?" He

dragged two more posts from the truck. They landed with a thump beside the growing pile.

"The home improvement store donated them." Used to hauling feed and mucking pasture, unloading the truck still had her out of breath. "It doesn't seem right you giving so much. It's not even your own child in the program."

About to drag the last two posts from the truck, he froze. Just for an instant, then he dragged them off the flatbed and hurled them to the ground. One of the peeler cores jolted off the pile, striking a rock and splitting in two.

"Damn." He pushed away from the truck, strode a few yards away. He stared off into the trees.

Sara ran back over what she'd just said, tried to understand what might have upset him. Tension clustered in her belly, a familiar anxiety. Men got angry, then they lashed out. For a moment, she couldn't catch her breath.

When he turned, she had to squelch the urge to run. But there was nothing in his neutral expression to confirm her irrational fear.

She forced herself to smile. It felt stiff on her face. "I do appreciate the donation."

He reached for the first of the rolls of wire fencing. "They were just lying around my place. I didn't have a use for them anymore."

Sara sensed a message in his words, but she wasn't about to press the issue. Whatever he'd intended the peeler cores for originally, it was none of her business. "I have forms in the house. So you can deduct the donation from your taxes."

"No, thanks." He dropped the roll of wire and started

back toward his flatbed. He held his shoulders so stiffly, Sara didn't have to touch him to know those muscles would be rock-hard under her hand.

Even without the knowledge of what might be eating away inside of him, empathy welled inside her. That emotion was safe enough. It was the kind of feeling one friend might feel for another. He was a stranger to her, but she responded to the kind of pain she sensed within him. She was only being human.

That she yearned to throw her arms around him, stroke his back to soothe him…that was another matter entirely. That was how Victor had snared her, playing on her sympathies, acting the wounded beast. In the end, she discovered he wasn't so much wounded as just a beast. She wouldn't let herself fall into that trap again.

He needed her to leave. He needed some space, some time to suppress the twist of grief that had surged up unexpectedly. Sara's innocent comment about not having a child in her program had just hit him wrong, a shot out of the blue he hadn't seen coming. She couldn't have known he'd intended to build a play structure for Christopher with these posts. If she'd just back off for a few minutes, he'd have himself under control again.

But she stayed, watching him wrestle the other three rolls of fencing from the truck, questions in her beguiling hazel eyes. Questions he wasn't about to answer.

As he leaned against the last roll, ruthlessly tamping down his grief, she gazed out at the rolling pasture. She had freckles across her cheeks, a consequence of the red hair, he supposed. He wondered how they'd feel under his fingertips.

"I was thinking—" she scanned the pasture "—if you fenced the pasture into two sections, I could keep the horses on one side while you build the paddocks on the other."

Wisps of auburn hair had come loose from her ponytail and they curled around her brow. What would those curls feel like against his palm if he smoothed them back?

She gestured toward the blackberry bushes. "It's narrowest there. If you start at the gate and dig post holes to the blackberries, the horses would still have enough space in the smaller section."

His sidetracked brain had better get back on the right road or his post holes wouldn't have a chance of being straight. "Let me get the truck out of here." He turned away from her and climbed back into the flatbed. As he inched out of the pasture gate, then back around the arena, he glanced back at her. To his everlasting gratitude, she didn't follow him.

But she was still there when he got back with his one hundred foot tape measure and can of marking paint. Whatever craziness had him distracted by her, she seemed unaware and completely unaffected by it herself.

She walked with him into the field, taking the end of the measuring tape when he handed it to her. "You and Jameson must be good friends."

"He got me out of a bind last year." Moving along the line she'd indicated, he drew an X at ten feet. "Kept me solvent when a client went bankrupt."

"Did you know him before…" A faint flush rose in her cheeks.

"Before he went to prison? Yes." Giving the tape measure case a little tug, he backed from his mark. "Everyone knew about Jameson."

She kept hold of the other end, keeping pace with him. "Have you always lived here?"

As he painted the next X with the fluorescent orange, he narrowed his gaze on her. "You planning to write the story of my life?"

"I don't mean to pry. I just…" She clamped those soft lips shut, then bent her head. As he cranked in the tape, he realized if she hung on, he'd have her reeled in and close.

But she let it go, staying the ten feet away, gazing off toward the berry vines. He studied her, for the moment not fighting the distraction. She certainly wasn't what you'd call a skinny woman, not one of those rail-thin model types you worried had anorexia or something. She had curves where women should have curves and hips a man could cup with his hands.

She also had a brain and spirit and he could see both when she swung her head around toward him. "You have a place here. I don't. I just wanted to know…" She shook her head. "Never mind." She turned on her heel and headed out of the field.

He was absolutely not going after her. If she had something stewing inside her, it was her own business. He had plenty on his plate to handle. He wasn't about to borrow any from her.

He thought she'd go hide out in her house, but instead

she went to the arena where the old lame gelding stood with his head over the rail. She rubbed the chestnut's face, leaning in as if conspiring about the shortcomings of men.

He was burning daylight mulling over what she might be saying. Impatient with himself, he measured out the next ten feet, marking the spot before moving on to the next. He didn't look at her again and so wasn't sure when she left, no doubt to head for her small house.

But damned if he didn't miss her when he noticed she was gone.

Sara peeled the last of the address labels from the sheet she'd run through her printer and stuck it on the flyer on her desk. Between local businesses and previous contributors to the program, she had nearly a hundred flyers ready to go out in the mail.

Adding the flyer to the stack, she glanced out the window above her desk to check Keith's progress. She might try to tell herself she only wanted to know when he'd be done, when the din of the excavator would stop. But she knew better. Her gaze had drifted to him again and again as her hands went through the motions of pressing address labels to flyers.

From this distance, she could barely make out the piles of newly turned dirt where he'd already drilled holes. The brush obscured the deep red soil, and she'd lost count of how many times he'd moved the Bobcat from one orange X to the next. Was he on his ninth hole? Tenth?

Picking up the stack of flyers, she evened their edges and secured the bundle with a rubber band. This was her first fund-raiser; up until now, she'd relied on Lydia Heath's largesse and the occasional individual who sent in a donation from the Rescued Hearts Web site. It had been Dani's idea to ask local businesses to sponsor a horse and then acknowledge the businesses with an ad in the *Marbleville Gazette*. The tiny weekly was glad to donate the ad space.

Raising the auger from the hole it had just punched in the ground, Keith maneuvered the excavator to the next mark in the dirt. He was nearly to the blackberry bushes, so he must be on the last couple. Good thing; it was past feeding time for the horses and they'd become restless in the arena.

No more restless than she felt watching Keith work. From her vantage point in the corner of her bedroom she'd carved out for her office, she couldn't make out the play of muscles in his arms and across his back, but she could imagine them all too easily. The stack of flyers bent in her hands as the fantasies unreeled in her mind.

Shoving back her wheeled chair, she rose from the desk with a huff of impatience. She felt like one of those women in the diet soda commercials, lusting after a well-built stud. It was a bad idea—no, a rotten idea to even consider Keith Delacroix in such blatantly sexual terms.

A chair wheel had caught on her capacious canvas handbag and when she tried to remove it, half the contents spilled out. As she gathered up the scattered items and re-placed them, her hand fell on a pink plastic packet of birth control pills.

She'd taken them regularly during those months with

Victor and for a few months after, strictly out of habit, certainly not because of need. In the aftermath of Victor's brutality, an intimate relationship with a man was out of the question.

Until now. Some perverse demon nudged her to open the plastic case, to count the two weeks of pills still remaining. These were certainly expired—she'd forgotten they were still floating around in her bag. It was the wrong time in her cycle to start them anyway. But temptation whispered naughty suggestions in her ear, temptation in the shape of Keith Delacroix.

So preoccupied with the pink plastic case, she didn't notice that the noise of the tractor had quit. It wasn't until she heard the rap on her front door that she realized Keith had finished and had come looking for her.

He couldn't see her there with the birth control pills in her hand, but she jumped nonetheless. Quickly tossing the case toward the trash, she scooped the rest of the miscellaneous junk into her purse, then hurried to answer the door.

Good God, he'd taken off his shirt. He stood there, bare-chested, shoulders seeming almost too wide to fit inside, T-shirt wadded in his hand. Sweat sheened his skin. The size of him set off alarm bells of fear in her, fear that warred with a very feminine lust. Her home's small foundation seemed to shift as she stared at the perfection of his body.

He rubbed at his forehead with the back of his hand and left a smear of dirt. Her fingers itched to reach up and rub the swath of red away.

"The holes are dug. I put a peeler core inside each one to keep the horses from stepping in them."

"Good." She stared at that red smear, balling her hands into fists. "Thanks."

"I can help you take the horses back into pasture." He rubbed the T-shirt across his face, wiping away sweat and the beguiling smudge of dirt. "Then I'd better get going."

If she'd thought he was dangerous on a Bobcat out in her pasture, it had been nothing to the peril he posed standing on her doorstep. She ought to ask him to leave, shut the door and hide in her bedroom. But her mother had ingrained in her a few lessons in courtesy before she died.

She stepped slightly aside from the doorway. "Can I get you something to drink?"

He hesitated before he answered, his gaze flicking down to her mouth before settling back on her eyes. "My boots are dirty."

"Leave them on the porch."

He bent to loosen the laces, giving her a view of his back that stole the breath from her lungs. It took everything in her not to press her palm against those shifting muscles.

Toeing off the boots, he stepped inside and she shut the door. Her living room with its oddly angled walls was barely large enough for the sofa and easy chair she'd bought at the thrift store, the end tables and television stand filling in what space the larger furniture didn't. Adding Keith into the mix made the room shrink.

She edged her way toward the kitchenette opposite the living area, past the retro fifties dinette table with its two red vinyl chairs. The dinette had been a real find at the Hart

Valley Hospice thrift, even with the small tear in one of the chair backs.

As she slipped into the kitchen, he followed, stopping by the dinette. "Who built your house?"

"A friend of Jameson's, I think. It was already here when I came for my first interview."

"A kit home, looks like."

"It's taken some getting used to, living in an eight-sided house."

Scanning the shallow angles of the walls appraisingly, Keith nodded. "Builder did a nice job."

Nice was that broad chest with a sprinkling of hair across it, the trail of soft curls leading to the waistband of his jeans. Sara yanked open the fridge and ducked her head inside. "Water, diet cola, iced tea…?"

"Iced tea would be great."

The chill of the refrigerator didn't seem to cool her. Grabbing the plastic pitcher of tea, she shut the door and set the pitcher on the tile counter. "Do you need anything to sweeten it with?" She looked back over her shoulder at him.

Shouldn't have. His gaze on her was so intense, she thought she'd melt from its heat. She was afraid to reach in the cupboard for a glass, afraid her fingers couldn't hold it.

His hand stretched toward her slowly and she turned, her first impulse to back away, put more space between them. But instead she drew nearer, just a step, enough that he could reach her.

She felt his touch, light as a breeze, in her hair. "More hay?" she asked, her voice a bare whisper.

He shook his head, his palm still brushing lightly against her hair. His blue eyes had darkened, seemed almost navy against his tan face. The featherlight weight of his hand sent sensation simmering down her spine and she wondered how long before her knees gave way.

Then he yanked his hand back and strode away from her into the living room. *"Damn."* He flung the T-shirt across the small room and it snagged briefly on a lamp shade before it fell to the floor. His back to her, his shoulders were taut with tension.

At a loss, Sara opened the cupboard and pulled down a large glass tumbler. Hands shaking, she filled it with ice, then poured tea into it. She had a lemon in the fridge, but she didn't think she could slice it without cutting herself with the knife.

She held the glass out toward him. "The tea's ready."

"Thanks." He moved to retrieve his T-shirt, pulled it on before returning to the kitchen. "I'll take some sugar if you have it."

Setting the glass on the dinette table, she went for the sugar bowl and a spoon. He took them from her, thankfully avoiding contact.

He spooned two heaping measures of sugar into the glass, then stirred. The clank of metal against glass clamored in the quiet room.

She couldn't stand the silence. "I'll get that receipt for those peeler cores. For your taxes."

He drained the iced tea. "No need. Could I get another glass?"

Mechanically she picked up the pitcher, refilled his glass. "It's no trouble. I have the paperwork in my office."

He shrugged as he doctored the second glass of tea. "If you want." He drank half the glass, then rolled the icy tumbler across his forehead.

She squeezed past him, glad of the respite from his presence. But she hadn't gone three steps down the hall before she realized he'd followed her.

"One bedroom, one bath?" he asked.

"Yes. My bedroom doubles as an office." She stepped into it, grateful when he waited at the door.

His gaze roved over every feature of the bedroom, from its ceiling fan to its double-paned window overlooking the arena and pasture. He barely glanced at the queen-size bed at one end, its covers for once pulled up neatly.

Sara opened the filing cabinet at random, completely at a loss as to where she'd put the donation receipts. "You can fill in whatever amount you think is reasonable for the fence posts."

As she opened the third drawer, he stepped into the room. Why a man in a grubby T-shirt, with dusty jeans and the shadow of a beard should look so darn appealing she had no idea. But her mind had gone completely blank with him now only inches from her.

"Looks like you didn't quite make the trash with this." He bent to the floor and to her horror, straightened with the plastic case of birth control pills in his hand.

She didn't need to see her face to know she was beet-red. Her cheeks grew hotter when she saw the recognition in his face. He knew exactly what he held in his hand.

Grabbing the case from him, she dumped it in the trash. "I'll have to get you a receipt later."

"Don't bother."

"They're here someplace." She had to get him to leave before she did something stupid. "I'll give it to you tomorrow."

He didn't budge. "I don't need it."

Get out, you crazy man, before I kiss you! She stood stunned, but old Dudley came to the rescue, screaming out a complaint, giving her the perfect excuse to give Keith the bum's rush. "I need to feed the horses."

He turned to leave. "I'll help you get them moved."

She followed him into the hall. "I can handle it myself."

He set the iced tea glass on the dinette table on his way to the front door. "Two can do it quicker."

Outside, he sat on her concrete steps to pull his boots back on. Sara racked her brain for an excuse to get him back in his flatbed and out of there, but she came up empty.

She made sure she wasn't too close as they headed for the arena. Dudley and the alpha mare, Shadow, anticipating their evening feed, trotted back and forth by the gate, nipping at the other horses.

She and Keith had left the halters on when they'd put the horses in the arena, so it was just a matter of clipping lead ropes on. "If we lead Dudley and Shadow, the others will follow."

So she took Dudley's rope and Keith took Shadow's. The other four horses waited until the lead gelding and mare cleared the gate before they trotted after. Pearly stopped to snag a clump of grass, but it didn't take much urging to encourage her to join the band in their field.

Halters hooked on the fence, Sara headed for the tractor she'd filled with feed earlier. While she started up the tractor, Keith returned to the excavator and drove it around the arena back to the flatbed. As she filled buckets with pellets and tossed flakes of hay into the pasture, he pulled the Bobcat back onto the truck.

She ought to be relieved he was about to depart, not disappointed. He really didn't need to do more than wave from his truck as he pulled out of the yard. She'd see him tomorrow anyway. Then, once he'd finished his work here, he'd just be another of the locals she greeted when she saw him in town.

Driving the tractor back toward the feed room, she watched him from the corner of her eye. He was giving the chains he'd secured the Bobcat with a pull, testing their tightness. Any second and he'd be climbing into the flatbed's cab.

The tractor parked, she shut off the engine and rounded the tack room so she'd be able to wave back as he left. Except he wasn't leaving. He was headed her way, closing the distance between them with long strides.

"About the barn," he said as he reached her. "I talked to my concrete guy. He'd be willing to come pour you a foundation when you're ready."

"I appreciate you looking into it."

Still he stood there, as if he'd forgotten he was supposed to leave. "You might think about where else you might need concrete. He'll probably have extra."

She wanted to tell him there wasn't anything else, that he should just go. But she had to think about what the program needed, not what she wanted. "We could use a wash rack over by the tack room. A concrete pad for that would be great."

He nodded. "About the barn—you have any of the materials lined up with Jameson?"

"He wants me to involve the community more. But it's tough arranging donations when I'm so busy with the program."

Another nod. "I'll talk with my suppliers, see what I can come up with."

"Why would you want to do this?"

For a moment, he seemed at a loss to answer. He glanced away, then back at her. "Because I can. Because it's what I know how to do. I can't teach those kids like you do. But I know how to work with my hands."

Something in his eyes tugged at her heart, a longing she would never have expected in such a no-nonsense man. "Thank you," she said softly. "For the work you're doing. For bringing Grace."

His jaw tensed. "See you tomorrow, then." He took a step away.

"Keith—"

He stared at her, his expression unwelcoming. As if he knew what she was about to ask.

"About Grace…if there's anything you can tell me—"

"No more questions. About me, about Grace." His voice was cold. "I'm done talking about the past." Then he turned and strode toward his truck.

Chapter Four

What did it matter if he wanted to keep to himself? It would be better for her anyway. The less she knew about him, the less he'd feel a part of her life. She'd only asked him what she had because she'd never abandoned the notion that some day she'd belong to a place as Keith did. Although she'd only been in Hart Valley for eight months, she'd begun to think that this could be home to her.

A week after she'd finally finished her MS in counseling at Sac State, she'd been lucky enough to come across Jameson O'Connell's ad. *Counselor wanted for children's program,* the ad in the *Sacramento Bee* had read. *Living accommodations on site. Must be experienced with horses.* As impressed as Jameson had been with her academic credentials, her stint at a dude ranch, at the time just a source of income for her and Ashley, proved to be the clincher.

Keith's flatbed truck had disappeared down Stony Creek Road, the dust on the driveway taking its time settling. The horses, busy with their evening feed, didn't so much as raise their heads as the sound of the big diesel engine faded.

She ought to go in and get her own dinner. She'd gulped down a carton of yogurt and an apple at lunch, too busy riding herd on the kids to eat much. She should be ravenous, but the unsettling day had stolen her appetite.

Maybe she'd throw together a salad and catch up on the newspaper. She had the Sunday edition of the *Sacramento Bee* delivered and had picked up the daily *Sacramento Bee* in town. She hadn't so much as opened the front page since the weekend.

Bag lettuce, some olives and tomatoes, cubes of cheddar tossed with balsamic vinegar would at least fill her stomach. She had a hunk of French bread left, too.

As she sat at the dinette, the newspaper spread out, the large bowl of salad at hand, her mind wandered back to Keith. She wasn't exactly eager to share the details of her own life, but she couldn't help but wonder what had gone so wrong in his that he didn't want to talk about it.

She fished the sports section out of the paper, wanting to check on how the Rivercats were doing in the minor league baseball stats. On the front page below the fold, there was a photo alongside a story about a three car collision at a stock car race. The crowd along the rail stared avidly out at the track.

Her heart froze solid in her chest. The picture was blurry, the face indistinct…it couldn't be him. He was dead, long dead and buried. She'd seen the item on the news five years ago.

They'd positively identified the body…hadn't they? She struggled to remember. They'd shown his picture during the newscast, but it had been an old one, a mug shot from one of his many arrests. The body had been burned pretty badly.

She stared harder at the photograph. The way Keith had turned things inside out for her, she wasn't thinking straight. The man in the picture resembled her father, but truly it could be anyone. She shouldn't jump to conclusions.

The phone rang and she jolted to her feet, knocking the chair to the floor. She almost couldn't pick up the phone, she was shaking so badly. When she saw her sister Ashley's number on the caller ID, relief flooded her.

"Hey, how are you doing?" Sara said, keeping her voice steady. She flipped the newspaper facedown. No point in frightening her sister with crazy speculation.

"I'm absolutely fantastic," Ashley said with characteristic ebullience. "Finals are finished, I have one last project to complete for one of my professors, then I'll be spending the summer helping out at Head Start."

"So you're still set on teaching? The first year of the program didn't scare you off?"

"I love it. I'm so looking forward to my own classroom."

"So, how's your social life?" Sara asked.

Ashley laughed. "What's a social life? How are things going at the ranch?"

"Busy, but great." Sara chattered on about the kids and the horses and her difficulties with some of the parents, avoiding any mention of Keith. Why would she bring him up anyway? He was just one of the neighbors, helping out around the place.

Once she said her goodbyes to Ashley, she picked up the newspaper again. The dateline of the story indicated the accident took place in Southern California. More than four hundred miles away, in an entirely different universe than Hart Valley.

It couldn't be him. It wasn't him. Sara was certain of it. Her father was dead, killed in a house fire five years ago. She and Ashley were safe.

She had more pressing issues to focus on than the un-lamented death of an evil man. Her students and their progress in the program this week. Her elderly horses' health and welfare. Successfully raising community funds for Rescued Hearts.

Dealing with Keith.

She crumpled the newspaper and walked it to the trash. She wished she could dispatch the clutter of emotions inside her as easily. Wished she could put the lid on her feelings for a man she had no business feeling anything for.

Appetite gone, she dumped her salad on top of the newspaper and headed for her office. Facing the mountain of paperwork waiting for her was the last thing she wanted to do. But better that than face her loneliness.

* * *

By Thursday, Keith had set the line of poles in concrete and had started running the wire fencing along them. Sara had done her best to ignore him out in the pasture, keeping her back to him as she worked with the kids. If her attention drifted to him, she snapped it back immediately, irritated with herself at shortchanging her students.

She was distressed, as well, with her lack of progress with Grace. The little girl still resisted interacting with the other children, stood passively waiting for direction, following every instruction seemingly without the least interest in the proceedings.

Yet Sara had seen Grace's muted excitement when she arrived in the morning, had seen at least a flicker of eagerness to get started with the day. Even if Sara hadn't made any inroads into Grace's inner self, that faint delight she revealed being around the horses might be the only thing that passed for happiness in the child's life.

Sara knew she would be pushing the issue with the next exercise. For the most part, she'd not demanded any more engagement than Grace offered. She allowed Grace's silence, letting the little girl move at her own pace.

But with only one more day of camp, Sara decided to up the stakes. At worst, it would achieve nothing; at best, she might achieve a breakthrough.

Uncertain and anxious, she couldn't help herself—she turned toward the pasture, seeking out Keith. He wrestled with a roll of wire, stretching it from one post to the next. As if he sensed her watching him, he looked over at her. She ought to be relying on her own strength, had to face this situation on her own. Still, that brief visual contact eased some of her tension.

Her assistants had untacked the horses and three of them stood in the crossties by the tack room. The other two, Pearly and Sable, remained in the arena, their lead ropes loosely looped over the rail. Their saddles hung on the top rail, bridles draped across them.

Another glance over her shoulder at Keith told her he'd ambled toward her, whether to ask a question or just watch, she didn't know. Sara locked her gaze with his briefly and lifted her hand to stop his forward progress. He slowed, then stopped beside one of the arena's massive steel pillars.

The students were in groups of three, her long-haired assistant, Ryan, filling out the third for the second group. They stood in a line with arms locked, Grace in the center between Jeremy and Ryan. Everyone but Grace smiled as they waited for instruction from Sara.

"The person in the middle is the brain," Sara told the kids. "The ones on either side are the brawns. Only the brain can speak and give directions. Only the brawns can carry out the directions."

The students giggled, exchanging grins. Grace stood frozen, her face set.

"The helpers have tacked up your horses for you for four days now. It's your turn to give it a try. But remember, the brains tell the brawns how to do it, the brawns carry out the instructions."

Even more laughter as the linked line of students walked over to the saddles. Grace moved along with Jeremy and Ryan, but her feet dragged in the dirt. The groups stopped at the rail where the horses' tack had been hung.

Marisa, the talkative nine-year-old acting as brain in the other group, gave out instructions in a loud, raucous voice. Despite seeing the horses saddled several days in a row, it wasn't easy for Marisa to explain how to pick up the saddle and place it on the patiently waiting Pearly. After one false start where the saddle ended up on backward, Marissa's team managed to get it properly positioned.

Grace's team still stood waiting. The little girl stared fixedly at the saddle, agony clear on her face. If she could have willed that piece of tack to rise from the rail and set itself on Sable's back, she would have. What she wouldn't do was speak.

On the other side of the arena, Keith watched, his shoulders taut, hands gripping the rail. Hefting himself up, he jumped the rail and started toward Grace. Sara set an interception course, catching him before he'd gone very far.

"Leave her be," she said softly.

"You don't know what she's been through."

He took another step and she put up a hand to stop him. She didn't want to feel the warmth of his skin through his T-shirt, the dampness indicating his hard labor. But there was no way she would let him proceed.

"No, I don't, because no one's told me anything, least of all, Grace herself. Care to enlighten me?"

He didn't answer. She hadn't expected him to.

Marisa's group had the cinch done up partway and now struggled with the bridle. Grace still stood stock-still.

Sara had put the little girl through enough. "Jeremy, switch with Grace. You're the brain now."

Grace sagged with relief and quickly traded places with Jeremy. Voluble Jeremy launched into a series of convoluted instructions that Grace happily followed, the ghost of a smile on her face. Despite the reprieve, the tension that never seemed to leave the little girl's body remained, as if she constantly waited for the next blow.

Keith turned away and retraced his steps across the arena, shoulders held as rigidly as Grace's. There was a common thread to the pain they both felt, Sara was sure of it. That neither one would share it with her frustrated Sara to the point of irritation.

Not that she'd ever take her annoyance out on Grace. Keith, on the other hand…

With a glance back to see that her helpers had the students well in hand, she followed Keith. He'd just slipped back through the rails when she caught up.

"Keith." She waited for him to stop, his back to her. "You can't interfere with the lessons."

"Sorry." He started off toward the pasture again.

She could have cheerfully strangled him. Stepping through the rail, she trotted to his side. "You two have a history. You'd rather keep it to yourself. I have no interest in intruding, but if it would help Grace—"

"I don't know anything." He grabbed the roll of wire fencing he'd been installing on the posts. "You'd better get back."

Unwrapping the stiff wire, he pulled it to the next post. Sara remembered how awkward the job was, stretching the heavy fencing, holding it in place while she drove the staples. "Class is nearly over. If you wait I can help with this part."

He dragged the roll into place. "Still have to take Grace home."

"I have iced tea in the fridge. Once you get back, we'll have a couple glasses, then get to work."

Broad hands gripping the wire, he didn't answer. Ryan called over to her, asking what next. She shouted back, "Time to untack. Be down in a sec."

His wide shoulders could have been fashioned of iron. "I don't know."

At first she thought he meant he wasn't sure he wanted her to help. But then he fixed his gaze on Grace leading Pearly from the arena.

Pain made his face harsh. "I don't know why she won't talk."

"Fair enough," Sara said quietly. "Do we have a plan on the fence?"

"Sure. I'd appreciate the iced tea."

As he wrestled the roll of wire into place, Sara headed down to the tie racks where the horses had been led. As the students groomed and combed and cleaned feet, the parents started arriving. A half hour later, the place was quiet again, with Keith on his way to take Grace to her sitter's, both of her helpers gone.

As Sara considered what had happened with Grace in the arena and her brief conversation with Keith, she realized this week would likely end with little or no progress with the little girl. To some extent, it had been an interlude for Grace, had given her something to focus on besides her pain. But whatever grief the little girl suffered, she'd hidden it so deep, five days weren't nearly enough to unearth it.

Entangled in her disappointment was the confusion of emotions she felt around Keith. Despite his insistence to the contrary, he was key to what was buried inside Grace, Sara was certain of it. But there wasn't a chance she would be able to get to an understanding of Grace through Keith.

The horses dozing in the arena, Sara turned toward her cabin to get the promised iced tea. There were cookies in the cupboard, as well; she might as well bring those out, too.

The tea in a plastic jug in one hand, cookies and a couple of unbreakable tumblers in the other, she headed back outside to wait for Keith. She didn't let herself think about how much she looked forward to his return, her anticipation of working with him. It would be bad enough becoming emotionally involved with Grace. Opening herself up to Keith would be an even greater calamity.

While Sara held the fencing wire in place against the last post, Keith shot staples into the peeler core with his nail gun. They'd managed the job of running 150 feet of fencing quicker than he'd thought they would. It was barely six and other than moving the gate from its current location, they had the fence complete.

They worked well together, maybe too well. She'd picked up on his rhythm, would pull the wire tauter before he'd asked her to, would stand exactly where he needed to give him space to drive home the staples. She'd grab another strip of brads even before he realized he needed them, had them ready for him when the gun emptied.

Of course, no matter how much room she allowed for him to work, it was never enough to keep his fantasies at bay. How a woman who'd worked out in the sun all day and labored with horses and children could smell so appealing he didn't know. A fragrance seemed to linger in her hair, along her skin. A soft floral scent that generated images of cool sheets and hot sex.

Entirely inappropriate images. Misplaced and unwanted. He was at the ranch to work, she was at his side to help. He doubted his wandering thoughts would be welcome.

Keith pounded the last staple into the post, then stepped back to survey their work. "You want me to move the gate now?"

They'd reuse the existing gate for the reconfigured pasture. He planned to do another run to the building and ranch supply for more posts and gates.

She swiped the back of her hand across her forehead. "It can wait until tomorrow. I'm desperate for a shower."

So was he, especially if she was there with him. She must have seen something in his face, because her cheeks flushed and she looked away.

Picking up the empty plastic jug and half-full package of cookies, she started down the fence line. "You want something to drink before you head out?"

All the iced tea in the world wouldn't quench his thirst.

He wanted to drink from her mouth, taste the salt of her skin. He felt ready to incinerate from the heat inside him.

No would be the right thing to say. But he didn't seem to know how to behave lately. "That would be great. Just give me a minute."

As he unplugged the nail gun and started coiling the extension cord he'd run from the arena, he watched her walk away. Although she'd protected her legs by pulling on jeans, her shoulders had reddened a bit in the sun. Maybe he ought to offer to smooth some lotion on her skin.

Maybe he ought to just walk to his truck and leave. Putting his hands on Sara, no matter what the pretext, was a phenomenally stupid idea. He might as well put a match to tinder during the summer fire season.

He'd intended to take the weekend off, had planned to try to get a few chores done at home. But maybe he ought to finish up here instead, not drag out this business with Sara any longer than he had to.

Detouring to his truck to put away the extension cord and nail gun, he took a look at his grubby jeans and wished he could go home and shower before he entered that neat little house of Sara's. But if he went home, he ought to stay there, not return for a glass of tea and Sara's company. That would be the safer course, with less pain for all involved.

He had a bottle of sanitizer gel in the truck and he gave his hands a spit and polish. As he slammed the pickup shut, he saw the magnetic sign reading Delacroix Construction had slipped on the door. He peeled it off and stared down at the plain lettering, black on white.

He'd fantasized once about adding "and Son" after the

Delacroix, had imagined Christopher working beside him in the business. He'd teach his boy how to wield a hammer and a power saw, how to frame a house, install windows, put up siding. Or maybe Christopher would have been sharper than his dad, would have gotten a law degree or an M.D. He'd been such a bright little boy.

Smoothing the sign back in place, Keith fought to set aside the ache inside him. He tried every year to blank his mind to the anniversary of Christopher's death, before the guilt could overwhelm him. He'd managed better some years than others. But with that other black day to struggle through only a month before then, he wasn't sure how he'd get through it this year.

He started toward the cabin, even more reluctant to face Sara again. The way she stirred things up inside him, she got him thinking too much, wanting too much. He wanted to tell himself it was just heat, just lust. But he couldn't deny the satisfaction he got working alongside her, building the fence.

He knocked on her door, then bent to untie his laces. He didn't want to track anything into her house, could be at least that civilized. He'd just shoved the second boot off when she opened the door.

An appealing pink colored her cheeks. "Sorry, I was on the phone."

When she stepped aside, he entered, resisting the temptation to brush against her. She'd cleaned up a bit; she smelled of soap and her hair spilled around her shoulders, freshly brushed. A few dark auburn locks lay damp and curled across her brow.

She swept one of those locks behind her ear. "I set the tea out. Help yourself."

"I'd like to wash up first." The slapdash cleansing he'd done in the truck wasn't enough.

"Bathroom's next to the bedroom."

Bad idea looking inside her bedroom as he passed it. Nevertheless, he took a peek, saw she hadn't made her bed. All the easier to fall into it with her.

Cupped hands full of icy water, he just about soaked his head. The soap by the sink smelled like her—another hazard—but he had no other choice but use it. The towel hanging on the rack was still damp, and he caught her scent once again as he buried his face in the terry cloth.

God, he was a mess. He'd better march his feet out of here, drive home, pay someone else to finish the work Jameson had asked him to do. He'd be better off shelling out the money than staying here one moment longer than he had to.

But when he stepped from the bathroom, saw Sara in her kitchen, her gaze off in the middle distance, he knew he wasn't leaving. He wouldn't be farming out the fencing to someone else, either. Foolhardy as it was, he wanted these last couple of days around her, couldn't quite convince himself to give that up.

As he approached, she smiled and pushed a filled glass of tea toward him across the breakfast bar. She had the sugar bowl out, a spoon beside it. The curve of her mouth looked sweet enough to taste.

"Thanks." He scooted the sugar bowl closer, glad they had the breakfast bar between them.

"I sliced some lemon, if you want it."

"This is good." He probably put too much sugar in his tea, but it seemed safer to focus on the spoon and stirring than Sara. "I could probably finish the paddocks over the weekend. Save me having to come next week."

Did he imagine the disappointment in her face? "I might not be around to help. I spend my weekends running errands."

The disappointment inside him was certainly real enough. But it would be better having her gone. "I can run fence on my own. Not as convenient, but I can manage." He set down his empty glass. "I'll get out of your way."

Turning toward the door, he took a breath to ease the tightness in his belly. The lonely evening stretched out before him, an agony he faced nightly, but still despised.

He heard her steps as she left the kitchen. "Keith." Her gentle voice soothed.

He faced her again. If all she had to say was "Thank you" or "I really appreciate your help," he didn't think he could stand it. He wanted more from her. He didn't even know what.

"Grace—"

"Closed subject." He edged toward the door.

"Wait, please…" He saw the pleading in her expression. "I haven't scraped even a millimeter below the surface with her. I need some way to reach her."

"It's Alicia's business. Not mine."

"Alicia suggested I talk to you."

Anger shot through him, tightening his hands into fists. "What did she tell you?"

Eyes wide, Sara took a step back. "Nothing. She just thought—"

"Grace is Alicia's daughter, not mine. What the hell would I know about it?" Except he did know. He knew plenty.

Sara stood her ground, chin lifted. "I don't know what you know. But I need some kind of insight. Please."

Grace's sad solemn face swam in his mind's eye. The way she'd hugged him that first day, the trust in her fragile soul—how could he just turn away from her?

He wasn't about to air his own dirty laundry. But maybe he could tell Sara a few things, what little bit he knew about Grace that didn't involve him. Maybe Sara would be able to assemble pieces of the puzzle he didn't even know fit together.

"Do you have plans for dinner?" he asked.

"A microwave meal and a can of fruit cocktail." The wry curve of her mouth intrigued him. "I'm not the world's most creative cook."

"How does Nina's Café sound? I can meet you there in an hour."

She tipped her head to one side, that soft auburn hair brushing her throat. "That would be wonderful."

Beyond wonderful. And completely idiotic. He was about to step into certain pain, hurt he swore he'd never again revisit.

Yet he couldn't seem to do a damn thing to stop himself.

Chapter Five

Seated in a booth near the front of Nina's Café, Sara tried to tuck her short-sleeved maroon V-neck more neatly into her black slacks, then made a halfhearted attempt to tame the hair that had sprung from her ponytail. It had taken her twenty minutes to decide how to dress for dinner, wanting her attire to be businesslike enough, but to not have the least suggestion of something appropriate for a date.

Because this wasn't a date. It was a meeting related to one of her students. The crazy emotions she felt around Keith had nothing to do with why she was here.

Sara glanced at her watch. Nearly seven-thirty. The Thursday night crowd had thinned considerably, all but a couple of the black vinyl booths were empty, and no one was seated at the tables arranged in the middle of the café.

Nina O'Connell, the owner, refilled sugar containers behind the counter. Lacey, the young twentysomething waitress who had brought Sara water and menus, chatted with Nina.

Lacey laughed at something Nina said, throwing her blond head back as she enjoyed the joke. Sara couldn't remember ever being that carefree. There had been those awful years with her father, then the weight of responsibility from age sixteen on. Moving from place to place to evade their father, the struggle to finish high school at night while taking care of her sister Ashley, the years of fitting in college between jobs so she and Ashley would have a future.

Ashley had done her part, working hard in school, scoring the good grades that brought her a lucrative scholarship at UC Berkeley where she was finishing her teaching credentials. But the past several months in Hart Valley had been the first time Sara felt able to take a breath.

She rubbed at her brow, exhaustion tugging at her. She'd really thought her nightmares had been a thing of the past. Her subconscious had fed her a steady diet of nighttime horror from age eight on, but it had been at least three years since the last one. She wasn't sure what the trigger was—the stress of the first week of camp, the way Keith had turned everything upside down for her, the picture in the *Bee*. Despite knowing the man in the photo wasn't her father, the reminder of him had apparently been enough to resurrect the bad dreams.

Wishing she could curl up in the booth and sleep, she took another look at her watch. Was he coming? Maybe

Keith had second thoughts about sharing whatever dark secrets he might know about Grace. Once he got home, away from her persuasion, he might have decided he'd just as soon keep it to himself.

Nina rang up a customer, then slipped into the kitchen. Sara could see Nina's husband Jameson through the passthrough, watched as Nina reached up to give him a kiss. Jameson put his arms around his wife, drawing her close, their kiss becoming more heated. Sara looked away, embarrassed, envious.

An older couple lingering over coffee were the last customers besides Sara. She wondered if she ought to go ahead and order. Anxiety over her meeting with Keith had stolen her appetite, but she'd better eat something. If he did show, she could ask Lacey to hold her order until his was in.

The door chimes jingled and Sara turned. Keith hesitated at the door although he spotted her immediately. Gorgeous enough in T-shirt and well-worn jeans, he looked incredible in tan khakis and dark brown polo shirt.

He started toward her, and her heart hammered in her chest. Traces of a familiar fear still lingered, his flash of anger in her living room still vivid. But joy crowded out the fear, the simple pleasure of seeing him again taking its place.

Neither fear nor joy were welcome. She needed clear-headed neutrality. This was about Grace, not her own muddled emotions.

He slid into the booth opposite her. "Sorry I'm late. Had a plumbing problem at a job site." He slid aside the menu and looked up as Lacey strolled over with her order pad.

"Long time no see." Lacey smiled, her pretty face lighting up. "How's Wyatt doing?"

"Fine. Busy." He handed over the menu. "Double cheeseburger with fries."

Sara ordered a turkey club, then waited until Lacey was out of earshot. "Wyatt?"

He downed half of his glass of water before answering. "My foreman."

Obviously disinclined to elaborate, Keith fidgeted with his water glass. His strong hands wrapped around the tumbler drew her gaze. She remembered the size of his fists during that moment of rage, how she'd wanted to run in reaction.

Still, she wished she had the courage to clasp his hand, to touch him without fearing that strength. But that contact was a double-edged sword. He'd already awakened old desires she would have thought Victor had completely obliterated. That heat could lead her back into the peril she swore she'd never put herself through again.

She ought to just cut to the chase, initiate the discussion of Grace and get it over with. They could eat their meal, part company, give her time to quiet the confusion inside her. But as wound up as Keith seemed, Sara sensed she'd have to pry the information from him.

Better to ease into the subject. "Has Delacroix been in business a long time?"

He set aside his water glass and locked his fingers together. "It's been thirteen—" his mouth compressed "—fourteen years."

"What did you do before?"

"I started in construction right out of high school. Worked my way up until I could start my own company."

"How many besides Wyatt work for you?"

He narrowed his gaze on her. "I thought we were here to talk about Grace."

So much for easing into it. "How long have you known her?"

"Does that matter?"

She felt like kicking him under the table. "It might. She's not been very openly affectionate, yet she hugged you the moment she saw you."

"I don't know what that was about." Picking up his knife, he turned it over and over in his hands. "I haven't even seen her for nearly a year."

"But she went to you so readily when she barely acknowledges anyone else, her mother included."

He flicked a glance up at her, then dropped his gaze to his restless hands. She waited, but he wouldn't look at her again.

Pulling teeth would have been a more delightful activity. "What was she like then? A year ago?"

"Her father had just died. What do you think she was like?"

Sara took a breath. "Then before her father died."

"She was—" he gestured with the knife "—a little girl. I really don't know what you want." Another glance up at her, then away.

"Was she quiet? Shy? Did she interact with other children or keep to herself?" Swallowing her reluctance to touch him, she grabbed his hand. "Do you care about her at all? Or do you dislike children so much you won't help this one child?"

* * *

Anger surged inside him, coupled with grief. Sara looked as if she wanted to run, but she maintained contact, her warm palm against the back of his hand. When he pulled away, he saw the relief in her face.

He picked up his water glass, but his throat felt so tight, he didn't think he could swallow. He set it down again. "Grace wasn't quiet. Wasn't shy. Sometimes she talked so much I thought my ears would fall off." He mustered a faint smile. "I used to tell her that."

Sara's next question nearly drove him from the table. "I take it you knew her father?"

She didn't know the history. It wasn't fair to resent that she'd asked him. He gave her a brusque nod. "For years."

"Was he a good man?"

No! He destroyed my life! His jaw tightened. Rob Thorne hadn't destroyed his life as much as he had Keith's illusions. "Rob was good to his daughter, if that's what you mean." A bitter taste had settled on his tongue. "He adored her."

Lacey returned and delivered his cheeseburger and Sara's sandwich. Keith was grateful for the distraction.

The young waitress smiled. "Tell Wyatt I said hi."

Lacey strolled off and Keith had the excuse of the greasy cheeseburger to avoid talking. He allowed himself the luxury of studying Sara, taking in the smattering of freckles on her cheeks, the shadows of her collarbone revealed by the V-neck top. He'd like to touch her there, run his fingertip along that angle of bone, up her throat, behind her ear.

His gaze locked with hers and her hazel eyes widened. Heat flared inside him, low in his body, and for a moment he forgot everything but the hitch in her breathing, her parted lips.

Forcing himself to look away, he caught the briefest glimpse of her breasts before focusing on his burger and fries. It had been a long time since he'd been with a woman, but that didn't excuse him leering at her.

She only nibbled at her sandwich, rearranged her French fries. Any minute, she'd start in again, grilling him about the past, trying to exhume memories he'd just as soon leave buried. He figured turnabout was fair play.

"Where were you before Hart Valley?" he asked before taking a huge bite of his cheeseburger.

"Here and there." She fidgeted with a fry, drawing circles in her ketchup.

He didn't feel inclined to let her off the hook. "Where?"

"I moved around a lot."

"In California?"

She dismantled one of the triangles of her club, picking out the turkey. "Mostly. A few places in Nevada and Oregon."

"What brought you here?"

She bit into the turkey, the motion of her mouth fascinating. When the tip of her tongue swiped a bit of mayo off her lower lip, the heat sparked inside him again.

"I finished up my masters in counseling degree at Sac State. Jameson had placed an ad in the *Sacramento Bee* for an instructor and ranch manager. Since I'd worked quite a bit with horses on the dude ranch, he thought I was a good fit for the job."

She pushed back her plate, although she'd barely eaten enough to keep a hummingbird alive. He swallowed the last bite of his burger. "Not hungry?"

She picked up another fry, but didn't eat it, finally dropping it back onto the plate. "I haven't been sleeping well."

He hadn't, either, the last few days, too wrapped up in fantasies of Sara, how he'd liked to touch her, kiss her. Despite the folly of it, his ego wished she felt the same. But from the shadows under her eyes, he sensed it wasn't him keeping her awake.

He could all too easily imagine lying in bed with her, holding her close and soothing her into sleep as he had his late wife, Melissa, the months after Christopher died. It was all he could offer at the time. Too little, he'd learned later. His comfort hadn't been enough for her.

Shaking off the old memories, he gestured to the waitress. "Go on home, then. I'll get the check."

She reached for her purse. "We'll split it."

He would have argued the point, but she already looked so tired. He pushed a twenty across the table toward her. "You can cover the rest."

They stepped from the café into the balmy evening. Most of the storefronts along Main Street were dark, the Hart Valley Inn and Sam's Saloon the notable exceptions.

She walked toward a small hatchback parked just outside Nina's. Keith stayed on the sidewalk, too tempted to touch her.

Opening the car door, she leaned over the top of it. "I appreciate what you've told me, but I don't know if it will get me anywhere with Grace."

"I don't know what else to tell you." What he did know wasn't anyone's business and certainly had nothing to do with Grace.

"I'm sorry." She pushed her bangs back, but the stubborn auburn strands popped back into place. "This isn't your fault. I just don't want Jameson to regret hiring me for the program."

"He won't." Keith would make sure of it.

She dropped her purse inside the car. "The other students are doing great. I've got Jeremy counting to five before he does anything with the horses. Better than the first day when he ran up and gave Sable's back end a big hug."

"Those kids are lucky to have you."

She sighed, her shoulders sagging. "Except Grace."

"Especially Grace." The urge to cross the short distance between them, to draw her into his arms, nearly overwhelmed him. He backed away a step. "I won't be staying when I drop her off in the morning."

Was that disappointment flickering in her face? "No problem."

"I have to dig the post holes for the paddocks next. The auger would be too noisy during the camp session."

"Of course. You've got the weekend for that." She got into her car.

He waited until she pulled out before heading for his pickup. The cheeseburger sitting a little too heavy in his stomach, the prospect of returning to his empty house adding to its weight, made it difficult to motivate himself to start his engine and drive home.

Turning the key, he backed onto Main Street, then

turned away from Interstate 80. Once out of Hart Valley, he turned on a small country road that wound its way to a secluded campground overlooking Deer Creek. The few lights of town left behind, only the headlights of his truck illuminated the darkness.

At the campground, he cut the engine and climbed from the cab. With the nearest busy road miles away, he heard only the burble of the creek and a soft breeze ruffling the pines. The utter blackness around him slowly eased as his eyes adjusted to the dim light of the half moon.

He made his way to a massive log above the creek's bank and lowered himself onto it. Years ago, those first months he held Christopher in his arms, he thought he might bring his son here. They'd get a tent, a couple sleeping bags, a Coleman stove. They'd catch rainbow trout in the creek and cook them up for dinner. They'd sit silently as deer approached and watch them drink from the bank.

Melissa had never been part of that dream. She'd declared herself a city girl who wouldn't know which end of the sleeping bag to climb into. She and Keith would lay together in bed, Christopher snuggled between them, laughing over the catastrophe their camping trip would be if she came along. *Bring me pictures,* she'd told him. *I'll enjoy it that way.*

They never had a chance for camping or for pictures. And Melissa's laughter stopped. Had her love for him ended then, too?

He hadn't come here to think about that. He didn't want to think at all. Drawing in a deep breath, he focused on the scent of pine, the rapidly cooling air, the rush of the creek.

If he could only absorb the peace here, take enough of it inside himself, then maybe he could live through another night.

Grace had been edgy and high-strung from the moment she arrived for camp on Friday. She seemed reluctant to climb out of Keith's truck, then looked almost frantic as his pickup drove away. When the little girl dropped a bucket of sweet feed she was helping Dani take out to Dudley in the newly fenced pasture, her eyes shone with tears. Tears she refused to let fall.

She didn't want to leave Dudley in the pasture, just hung her thin arms around the old gelding's neck as he munched his treat. When Dani finally coaxed her back to the tie racks where the other children were getting their ponies ready, she stood by the tack room, masked with grief. She stared longingly out at Dudley, ignoring Pearly who waited to be groomed and tacked up.

"Dani," Sara said. When the teen approached, Sara told her quietly, "Put Pearly away and bring out Dudley."

Dani stated the obvious. "Dudley's lame."

"He won't have to do a thing but walk. He does that much in the pasture." She glanced at Grace. "And she won't weigh much more than a flea on his back."

When Dani untied Pearly and turned the gray pony toward the pasture, fear flashed in Grace's face. She looked up at Sara, still silent, but the question clear—*I don't get a horse today?* She looked ready to run after Dani.

Sara put a hand on Grace's shoulder. "She's bringing Dudley for you."

Sara was certain the little girl would dissolve into tears.

She gulped in air, small hands fisted, and through sheer force of will, she kept the tears at bay.

As Dudley limped toward them, Grace wriggled with tension. Another look up at Sara, another silent question. "Go on, Grace. You can lead him the rest of the way."

She took off like a shot. Jeremy, grooming Sable within an inch of the old mare's life, piped up. "That's against the rules, Sara. She's 'sposed to always, always walk around the horses. You said."

She had told them that the first day. The point had been driven home to them Tuesday when Jeremy dashed toward Marisa's horse in a fit of energy. Shadow, the old thoroughbred, had spooked sideways, nearly unseating Marisa.

"You're right, Jeremy. I'll make sure to remind her."

By the time Dani and Grace had Dudley at the tie rack, the little girl had swung from abject sadness to an almost manic joy. She brushed the old gelding with exquisite care, scrubbing off every manure stain with the curry, combing every tangle out of his mane and tail.

The other students were long past ready, and Grace hadn't even gotten the saddle on her horse. Jeremy especially was bouncing with impatience and if Sara didn't occupy him soon, he'd explode from all his boundless energy.

In the end, Sara had Dani stay behind with Grace while she and Ryan took the other students into the arena. The little girl eventually joined them, and when she finally climbed on Dudley, her elation lit her face like a beacon.

As the day's activities proceeded, Grace did everything asked of her, even interacting with the other children, although with gestures, not words. When she teamed with

Jeremy in a ribbon race—at a walk in deference to Dudley's lameness—she clapped when they won. Sara wished fervently that Grace could have started the week like this. How much more progress they would have made by now.

During lunch, she sat with the other students for the first time, rather than beside Sara. She shared her brownies with Marisa and took one of Marisa's chocolate chip cookies in return. Her gaze often strayed to Dudley hanging out in the arena with his equine buddies.

Everything started to fall apart after lunch. Keith's return seemed to trigger Grace's tension again. When he pulled into the driveway, fencing supplies piled high in the back of his flatbed, the kids had just led their horses into the arena. Sara motioned to Keith to pull around to the pasture, telling the students to wait until he'd parked before mounting.

Grace stared at the flatbed, riveted, as it slowly made its way around the outside of the arena. Clutching Dudley's mane, she ignored Dani when the teen asked her to lead her horse to the mounting block. Grace stood frozen, still mesmerized by the flatbed as Keith cut the engine. The other four students had taken their turns at the mounting block and rode their horses along the rail, but Grace hadn't moved.

Triggered by Dani's silent plea for help, Sara crossed the arena to Grace. "Go help Marisa," Sara told the teen.

Grace hung on to Dudley's mane as if to hold her world together. Sara struggled to put the pieces together. She would have thought it was Keith that frightened Grace, but this morning, she wouldn't leave Keith's truck. Then she refused to ride Pearly, although in the course of the week, she'd ridden all the horses, the flea-specked gray included.

Dudley had been the one constant for Grace, the one she visited every morning when she and Dani fed the old gelding his medicine, the one she gave her last pats to when she left. She hadn't let herself attach to anyone or any horse…except Dudley.

Out of the corner of her eye, she saw Keith had come to the rail. She met his gaze and, with a gesture, invited him into the arena. He walked toward her, strong and solid in blue jeans and a T-shirt. So used to shouldering her own burdens, it would be such an incredible luxury to hand over responsibility to someone else for once. To Keith.

She wasn't sure how inviting him over would play out, but he was somehow key in Grace's distress. Maybe his presence would make things clear.

"Grace needs some help up on Dudley," Sara told him as he reached them.

He didn't ask, didn't question. He just locked his fingers, waiting for Grace to rest her bent right knee in his cupped hands. She hesitated, then released Dudley's mane and positioned herself for Keith's assistance. He easily lifted the little girl, holding her beside the horse until she got her left foot in the stirrup. Swinging her right leg over, she settled into the saddle.

"Go out on the rail with the other kids," Sara requested.

Grace complied, contented to be on Dudley's back. She still held her shoulders rigidly, her back ramrod straight. But for the moment, she'd grasped on to a little happiness.

Sara watched as Grace fell in behind Jeremy on Sable. "Any idea what's going on with her today?"

Beside her, Keith followed the progression of the horses along the rail. "What do you mean?"

Sara looked up at him. He wasn't any more relaxed than the eight-year-old riding Dudley. "Did something upset her this morning?"

He turned away from her, his gaze on the horses. "I have no idea."

"Did she seem unhappy when you picked her up at the sitter's?"

He finally faced her. "She's not a happy child."

"Any less happy, then?"

Hands shoved into his pockets, he shrugged. "She wouldn't get in the truck."

"Then wouldn't leave it when she got here." Sara caught Dani's eye, signaling her to have the students turn their horses around. "Wouldn't ride the horse I asked her to, was horrified when you turned up."

Keith narrowed his gaze on her. "You think I have something to do with this?"

"Tangentially." The answer clicked inside Sara. "It's not you personally. It's what you represent."

"What the hell does that mean?" He didn't loom over her exactly, and it was only irritation she could hear in his tone, but fear skittered along her skin.

Sara tamped it down impatiently. "You represent the end. Of camp. Of being around the horses. Of seeing Dudley every day. She hasn't wanted to take any step today that brought her closer to the end."

His head swung up as Grace came into view again. Her face was so solemn, as if she barely held sadness at bay. "Have you gotten through to her at all?" he asked.

Sara wanted desperately to say yes, but that would be a lie. "I thought there might be a breakthrough today. She seemed so much more fragile in a sense, I thought she might be willing to open up. But she needs more time."

Shifting, he crossed his arms over his chest. His flexing shoulders tempted her to touch. "Can she do another week?"

"Grace's therapist barely persuaded Alicia's insurance company to cover part of this week. Alicia hasn't got the wherewithal to pay for another week. And besides—" she glanced at him, then back at the horses "—there's still the transportation problem."

He stared down at his feet. She hadn't expected he'd speak up and volunteer, but she'd hoped he would none-theless. She couldn't keep the hard edge from her voice when she told him, "I have to get back to work."

"I'll go unload." He strode back across the arena.

She refused to watch his retreat. Her stomach a mass of knots, she felt anxious and heartsick all at once. The thought of letting that little girl go home today, just as bro-ken as when she arrived, hurt badly.

Sara went through the motions for the rest of the les-son, giving instructions by rote, fighting to remain neutral, to cut the ties she'd begun to form with these children. Jer-emy and Marisa were continuing next week, but the bal-listically active little boy and the chatterbox nine-year-old girl hadn't touched her heart like Grace had.

By the time the parents began arriving, Keith had unloaded his truck and pulled it into the parking area. She spoke briefly with the parents whose children wouldn't be returning, advising them she'd be sending a final report to their respective therapists. Jeremy's mother and Marisa's grandmother were both effusive in their praise of Sara's program, telling her how much progress they'd seen in their children in the course of the week.

They drove off, leaving only Grace. While the little girl went with Dani to say her goodbyes to Dudley, Keith sat in his truck, his cell phone to his ear. She should have been relieved he'd finish his work here Sunday, that she wouldn't have to see him here at the ranch after that. But as dispirited as she felt over Grace, the thought of Keith vanishing from her life set off conflicting emotions.

In the pasture, Dani had a comforting hand on Grace's shoulder as the little girl stroked Dudley's neck over and over. Sara could barely stand to watch her. She would have to find a way to bring Grace over here to visit the old gelding. That would be the least she could do.

Sara headed for her small house, intent on doing something for Grace here and now. She had two or three horse books she had as a child, the few possessions she'd managed to hang on to during her nomadic life. Maybe she'd offer them to Grace, loan them at least. Give her something to remind her of her week here.

She was in her bedroom, on tiptoes searching on a closet shelf when she heard the knock on the door. A quick glance out the bedroom window told her Dani and Grace were just now coming in from the pasture. Which meant her visitor was Keith.

Her feelings were in such a jumble, she wished she could ignore him and hide. But she couldn't let him leave with Grace without giving her the books.

Abandoning her search for the moment, she hurried to the front door. There he stood, broad shoulders, capable hands, questions buried in his blue eyes. After more than a decade of fear, she wished with all her soul for the protection of a man. This man.

When he leaned toward her and cupped his hands around her shoulders, fear sizzled away in a flash of heat. When he lowered his face to hers, she stretched up to meet him.

His kiss should have frightened her, should have reminded her of Victor's sometimes cruel mouth. But Victor had never been this tender, this gentle. Keith's kiss was a revelation, a fragment of joy. Long enough to assert itself, short enough that when he drew back she longed for another.

Then a rush of good sense washed over her and she stumbled back. Wiping her mouth with the back of her hand, she shook her head. "You can't—"

He looked stunned. "God, I'm sorry. I don't know what—"

"Grace is waiting for you." She'd have to find a way to get the books to the little girl later.

Stepping back from the doorway, he glanced toward his truck. He waved, no doubt at Dani waiting there with Grace. Good heavens, had they seen the kiss? Hopefully they had seen Keith lean in and nothing more.

"I'll be back tomorrow," Keith told Sara, his mask of impassivity in place again.

"I won't be here." She couldn't. She'd find somewhere else to be.

"Okay." He backed another step. "I'm sorry."

Turning on his heel, he walked away. Sara shut the door and sank to the living room carpet, hands over her face to stop the tears.

Chapter Six

As he worked on the paddocks over the weekend, Keith tried to tell himself it wasn't disappointment he felt at Sara's absence. He tried to convince himself her vanishing act was for the best, especially after his monumental misstep Friday afternoon. It would have been awkward seeing her, an embarrassment for both of them.

Better to have young Brandon Walker giving him a hand stretching fence instead of Sara. The fourteen-year-old son of deputy Gabe Walker was a hard worker, conscientious and responsible. Brandon had only been back in Gabe's life a year. They'd finally found each other a decade after Brandon had been kidnapped by his mother. Keith had been glad to help the boy make a few bucks over the summer.

But his mental lectures about Sara didn't keep him from checking for her hatchback over on the other side of the house where she usually parked it. They didn't stop him thinking about her a thousand times a day. And as foolhardy as it was, on Saturday, long after Gabe had picked up Brandon, Keith lingered until six, hoping to catch a glimpse of Sara returning to feed the horses. When her assistant Dani turned up instead and told him Sara had gone out of town for the weekend, he refused to let himself acknowledge the ache inside.

Instead he loaded his tools into the truck and headed into Marbleville for dinner at La Colina, blotting out all thoughts of Sara. But the feel of her mouth against his, her soft sighs, and the scent of her skin still crowded his brain. Not even a scorching plate of *chile colorado* could wipe away the images.

He still didn't know what had possessed him. He'd resisted touching her all week, had kept his distance as best he could. He kept himself focused on his work, his attention only occasionally straying to the auburn-haired woman in the arena below him. Having her work beside him on the fence had been tough, but he'd made it through without a stumble, and he'd thought he was home free.

Then she'd opened the door to him, literally, figuratively. The vulnerability in her face, its source no doubt her frustration and regret that she'd made no inroads into Grace's problems. He'd thought at first to offer a hug, comfort her that way. But once he reached for her, comfort became need and he was kissing her.

Sunday afternoon, all the fence up, only two more paddock gates to install, he and Brandon took a break with a couple of sodas. Every one of the few cars that zipped by on Stony Creek Road started Keith's heart pounding as he anticipated Sara's return. None of them slowed, none of them turned into the drive.

Seated on a boulder, Brandon downed the last of his cola. "Just two more gates left. No problem finishing today."

Except he didn't want to finish. Completing the task meant he wouldn't be seeing Sara anymore. "When's your dad picking you up?"

"Fifteen, twenty minutes. He's taking me into Sacramento to buy me a laptop." The dark-haired boy grinned, his green eyes bright. "I've never had my own computer."

His thoughts caught him unaware. Christopher would only have been eight, too young for a computer of his own. But Keith would have made sure his son had one at home, to use for his schoolwork, maybe play a few computer games. He'd been such a bright kid as a two-year-old. He would have taught Keith how to use the thing.

"Let's get going then." Keith set his soda can on the boulder beside Brandon's and they grabbed the next gate. Brandon held it in place while Keith bolted the hinge.

As Keith torqued the ratchet, a persistent sorrow gripped him. He kept imagining Christopher here instead of Brandon, his boy as strapping as Gabe's son, as willing a worker. Once they were done here, it would be him driving down to Sac, buying his son the latest computer with all the bells and whistles.

But his arrogance had destroyed that dream. He'd been

so caught up in his work, his attention on his latest project, Melissa's worry had seemed overblown. Money had been tight, too, and their medical insurance barely covered the basics. They took a big hit with every doctor visit.

It's just a bug, Melissa. He'll be fine. He would have given everything he owned, his very soul, if he could take those words back.

Gabe pulled into the ranch driveway just as Keith and Brandon finished the last gate. The deputy maneuvered his SUV into a parking space, then climbed out and waved. Keith waved back, but stayed put, not exactly in a social mood.

Brandon crushed the empty soda cans and set them beside Keith's toolbox. "Great working with you, Mr. Delacroix. If there's anything else this summer…"

"I'll let you know."

Brandon glanced over his shoulder at his father. "Can I help you put everything away?"

"I've got it. I'll cut a check tomorrow, drop it in the mail to you."

"Thanks. Bye!" He turned and trotted off, vaulting over the arena rail and cutting across toward his dad. Another wave from both Walkers, then they drove off.

Leaving Keith alone. He dropped the ratchet and leftover bolts into the toolbox, unplugged the power drill. Retrieving the extension cord, he carried everything to his truck and stowed it. Nothing else to do. No more reason to stay.

He couldn't face another dinner alone. It always seemed so pitiful, the only one at a tiny table, usually tucked away in a corner. No one to talk to during the meal, no one to share his day with. That kind of camaraderie had ended in his marriage long before Melissa's death. He'd had just a taste of companionship the other night at Nina's Café with Sara, had forgotten until then how much he enjoyed sharing a meal with a woman.

God, he wished she'd come back. He shouldn't even think it, let alone want it so much. But if he could see her once more before he left, maybe he could quiet the pain inside him.

Out in the pasture, five of the horses wandered and grazed, nibbling on what was left of the spring grass. The sixth horse, a liver chestnut with a broad white blaze, stood stock-still beside the blackberry vines. It leaned forward, straining a bit, then went still again.

Keith ducked through the arena rails, strode across the soft footing, then slipped through the pipe panel on the other side. Running up the slope toward the new pasture gate, he could see the gelding's back left foot stretched oddly out behind him. Once he was through the gate, he could see the liver chestnut had his back foot caught.

The horse stood patiently, waiting for rescue. A young, green horse might have thrashed and struggled, injuring itself in the effort to get free. This wise old boy understood he'd be better off waiting for a human to help.

As Keith pushed aside the berry vines to assess the problem, he heard the rumble of a car engine and the crunch of tires on gravel. For a moment, he forgot the horse's predicament, probably forgot his own name as Sara arrived. One hand on the gelding's withers, he watched Sara drive around the property to park her car on the far side of the small house.

She must have seen him in the pasture beside the horse. She was on her way toward him seconds after the car's engine shut off, running along the pasture line. In denim shorts and tank top, she was as luscious as the ripening berries behind him.

As soon as she got the pasture gate latched behind her, she called out, "Is Indy okay?"

He fought for breath to speak. "Fine. He's got his right hind caught."

She eyed him warily as she grew closer. "Good thing you were here."

He wanted desperately to reach for her, to touch her. "I don't think he's been trapped long."

As she edged around him, he drew in a breath, taking in her scent, struggling to keep the sensual images at bay.

She moved to Indy's rear to assess the situation. "He's wedged his foot between a couple of fallen tree limbs. Probably paying too much attention to the sweet green grass to notice the dead fall hidden by the blackberry vines."

He stayed by Indy's head, with the horse between him and Sara. He had the excuse of keeping the old gelding calm, but Indy was unconcerned, well occupied munching what grass he could reach. Still, Keith didn't know what he'd do if he had Sara within arm's length.

Sara tapped the gelding's right rear hock and Indy shifted his weight off that foot. So well trained, the horse didn't even flinch as Sara guided his ankle free of the dead branches. He moved away, stepping clear of the tangle of wood as he moseyed on toward the other horses, nipping grass along the way.

With the gelding gone, he and Sara were barely four feet apart. No more than a stride to reach her, an instant before he could put his hands on her, feel the warm skin of her arms.

He stepped away instead of toward her. "I was just leaving."

She caught up and walked alongside him toward the gate. "Do you have a minute?" Her expression was still wary, but determined.

He was pretty certain he didn't want to hear what she had to say. "I'm pretty beat." Not quite the truth since despite the hard day's work, just the sight of her had shot him full of energy.

She unlatched the gate. "I'd be glad to buy you dinner."

He couldn't let himself say yes. "A little early for me."

"Me, too. I need to unpack anyway, take a shower…"

Sara naked under a rush of hot water thrust into his mind. He focused on latching the gate behind him, trying to quash the images with the mundane chore. "What's this about?"

She didn't answer. He glanced over at her as they continued down toward the arena. Her head tipped down, she swept a lock of hair that had escaped her ponytail behind her ear. "I'd rather talk about it at dinner."

In another woman, he might have interpreted her evasiveness as an attempt to flirt, to draw him in. But with the space she maintained between them and the keep-away signals she sent off, he doubted she was being coy.

Which only emphasized the need to say no to her. Whatever she wanted to discuss, he'd be better off not hearing. "Dinner won't work. I've got too much to take care of at home."

They continued in silence to his truck. Pulling open the door, he was about to climb inside when he felt her hand on his arm, her touch brief. "Keith, please."

Turning back to look at her was a big mistake, but he did it anyway. There was no way he could resist the plea in her face. "Give me a couple hours."

She smiled and he thought his heart would burst in reaction. "Shall we meet at Nina's again?"

Sunday nights, the busybodies held court at the café, chewing over the week's scandals. He'd just as soon not be the main course. "How about Vincenzo's in Marbleville?"

"I haven't been there yet, but it sounds fine. What time?"

He tried to calculate how long it would take to get through the weekend chores he'd set aside to build paddocks. Laundry, a pile of dishes, at least a quick swipe with the vacuum and mop.

"How about you just come by my place?" Once the words were out, he realized it was a rotten idea. Sara walking around the rooms of his empty house would only make them lonelier when she left.

"Okay," she said, her tone a bit hesitant. "Just give me directions."

He scribbled his address and directions on the notepad he used for estimates, including his phone number. "That one turn is tricky. If you miss it, give me a call and I'll meet you at the main road."

He finally climbed into the truck and pulled out, tension tightening his shoulders until he'd reached Stony

Creek Road. His emotions kept their grip on him as he headed toward Interstate 80, and he nearly drove right past the familiar exit for Marbleville.

He'd agreed to dinner with her, despite his better judgment. Even worse, he was looking forward to it. What kind of lunatic was he?

Nearing the turn for Keith's house, Sara slowed on Cedar Ravine Drive and kept a sharp eye to the left. During her short time in the Hart Valley area, she'd been so busy getting the Rescued Hearts program up and running, she'd made few visits to Marbleville, let alone the surrounding area. She'd already made one wrong turn and ended up on a rutted old logging road. She didn't want to risk the suspension on her hatchback with another mistake.

She'd nearly passed the stout pine Keith's directions indicated would be at the end of his private road before she spotted it. Luckily traffic was light—which in rural Marbleville County meant not another soul in sight—so when she stomped on her brakes, there was no one behind her to honk and shake their fist. A big change from bursting at the seams Berkeley, where she'd spent the weekend with her sister.

Slowing to a crawl down Keith's gravel driveway, Sara rolled her shoulders in a vain attempt to shake loose the tightness. She'd hoped for a relaxing two days running her weekend errands with Ashley in the Bay Area, but she'd been sorely disappointed. Her sister was too busy to spare her much time, and buying the camp craft supplies and her own necessities at a packed shopping mall loaded on the stress.

Her escape from Keith and the aftermath of his kiss should have given her some breathing space, some perspective. But confusion still froze her brain, the questions still tumbling and crowding out clear thought. Why had he kissed her? What did it mean? Even more key—why did she enjoy it so much?

Her heart rattled in her chest at the memory and she felt so shaky, she pulled the car over. Keith's white ranch-style house lay just beyond the next bend in the road. She could see it through the tangle of oaks and pines. Just the thought of him so near sent her heart racing again.

Leaning back in the seat, she squeezed her eyes shut. She'd thought Victor had destroyed the ability in her to find pleasure in a man's touch, in his kiss. Other men had tried to breach that wall Victor's brutality had built, kind men, gentle men. But the fear stood in the way, chilling her inside.

Opening her eyes again, she stared through the trees, her emotions in conflict. She could turn around and go back home, call Keith and make her request over the phone. But that would make it far too easy for him to say no, and that answer was unacceptable. She required his cooperation, for Grace's sake. The troubled little girl's needs far out-trumped Sara's fears.

Putting the car back in gear, she continued down the gravel road and into the circular driveway in front of Keith's house. Her palms were a little sweaty and she wiped them on the camel colored slacks she wore. With the day's heat lingering, she'd wanted to wear shorts and a tank top instead of slacks and a sleeveless forest-green shirt. But thinking of this as a business meeting rather than a social call helped keep her rampant fantasies in line. Dressing in a businesslike fashion helped maintain that illusion.

As she shut off her engine, he stepped from the house, his gray khakis neat and sedate, his black T-shirt just a little bit dangerous. Sara didn't want to get out of the car, too afraid she'd touch him the moment he was within reach. But she was here for Grace.

By the time she opened her door, he was beside her car and she had to sidle out of the way to keep her distance. Her hands shook as she shut the door.

"Come on in." He gestured toward the house.

"I know you're tired. It might be better if we head straight for the restaurant." The wide front porch welcomed her with its redwood railing and cool shade. The rambling ranch-style house had everything she would have wanted in a home, but never had—from the vivid purple and luscious peach bearded irises in the front flower beds to the generous windows that would allow the sunset's coral and red glow inside.

"Actually—" he shifted his feet "—I found some chili squirreled away in the freezer. There's a box of corn bread mix and I picked up fresh strawberries from a stand up the road."

She remembered passing it and could imagine the tart sweetness in her mouth. But sharing a meal with Keith in the intimacy of his house… "I hate to put you to all that trouble."

He raked his fingers through his short hair. "It would

be less trouble than driving into town, dealing with the Sunday night dinner crowd at Vincenzo's. The chili's decent. I made it a couple weeks ago."

There was a swing on the front porch, cushioned with pads in a faded floral pattern. In all her life, she'd never sat on a porch swing and watched the sunset. An irresistible image sharpened in her mind—her and Keith on the swing, the sun sinking in an extravagant display of carmine and rose.

She looked up at him. "Can we eat on the porch?"

Surprise flickered in his face. "Sure."

"On the swing?"

"The pads probably need a good scrubbing."

"I'll take care of it." It was the least she could do.

His gaze narrowed, a faint smile curving his mouth. "I'll bring you out a bucket and a sponge before I get dinner going."

It was such a small thing, dinner on the front porch, but it made her happy. As Sara took the bucket of soapy water and a sturdy sponge over to the swing, she found her emotions surging over such a mundane chore. But home had always been a distant, unreachable goal. As much as she liked the small one-bedroom at the ranch, it didn't fulfill that need. Keith's rambling white house seemed like the missing piece of the puzzle.

They ate spicy chili and warm corn bread on the porch, the sun going down in a blaze of brilliant yellow and muted purple. Sara sat at one end of the swing, Keith leaning against the porch rail. She focused on her meal, the glorious sunset bleeding into a darkening sky, reluctant to voice her request during dinner. Keith didn't prod her, maybe just as disinclined as she to spoil the pleasure of the evening.

After they'd rinsed their dishes in Keith's homey country kitchen, Sara stalled even further by offering to bake shortbread for strawberry shortcake, one of the few things she'd learned to cook at the dude ranch. Keith disappeared down the hallway she assumed led to his bedroom as she threw together the ingredients, but returned just as she set the sweet biscuits into the oven. His expectant expression told her she couldn't delay any longer.

Leaning against the butcher block island, Keith seemed too large for the spacious room. Sara tucked herself in the corner between the oven and refrigerator, the waves of tension rolling off Keith skittering across her skin like electricity.

"It's about Grace," Sara finally said.

His expression shut down immediately. "I haven't got anything more to tell you."

She suspected he knew more than he was willing to say. "On my way home from the Bay Area, I made a couple calls. To Jameson. To Grace's mother."

He looked wary. "And?"

"Jameson is willing to sponsor Grace at camp for another couple weeks. Alicia is in agreement. There's only one unresolved issue."

Now he knew what she was about to ask; she could see it in his eyes. He had *no* written all over his face.

She stepped toward him, struggling to find the words to convince him. "I know it's a big imposition to drive her every day."

He just stared, his displeasure clear in the lines bracketing his mouth.

"You have a business to run, I know that. It's terribly inconvenient—"

"Inconvenience has nothing to do with it." His harsh tone sent a trickle of alarm up her spine. Yet there wasn't a shred of threat in his stance. He stood motionless, arms crossed over his chest. She was the one who had moved closer.

She was less than a foot away without even realizing it. Still, she stood her ground. "If I could find someone else, I would. But she's so fragile. She knows you. There's a connection between you."

His jaw worked, the tendons in his arms taut. "It's a bad idea, Sara."

"Maybe I could pay for your time. I can talk to Jameson—"

"I damn well don't need Jameson's money!" The angry words hung in the air between them. Dropping his arms, his hands tightened into fists. For a heartbeat, Sara froze in fear, waiting for the blow.

Apparently unaware of her reaction, he relaxed his hands, shoved them into his pockets. "I can't."

"Why not?" When he didn't answer, Sara reached over and rested just her fingertips on his arm. It wasn't as frightening as she thought it might be. "There must be a way—"

In an instant, his hands were on her shoulders, warm and strong. It should have terrified her.

"I can't," he whispered as he lowered his mouth to hers.

Chapter Seven

Fear clutched at her just for an instant as his lips pressed against hers, then washed away in a flood of sensation. Her hands lifted of their own accord and rested lightly against his chest. His heat warmed her palms, inviting her to explore the contours of his body.

His mouth moved across hers, more imperative than with his first kiss two days before, but still gentle. If he'd pushed her, ravaged her, thrust immediately with his tongue, she knew the fear would have taken hold. In that moment, his tenderness blotted out the old ugly memories, covered them with a veneer of pleasure.

He drew back, dropped his hands. "That's why," he said harshly, then strode out of the kitchen. Wrenching open the front door, he left the house, leaving her alone and chilled.

The oven timer beeped, tugging her from her daze. She had to open two drawers to find an oven mitt, then fumbled with the controls before she found the Power Off button. Heat surged from the open oven as she pulled out the sheet of shortcake, and she had to drop the pan in a hurry when a thin spot in the mitt made contact with the hot metal. It hadn't been long enough to burn herself, but she ran her hand under the cold water nonetheless.

At a loss as to where a cooling rack might be, she set the six shortcakes on a sheet of paper towel, then busied herself with washing and slicing the strawberries. She was just going through the motions, waiting for Keith to return. She didn't have a choice. One way or another, she had to persuade him to agree to transport Grace.

She'd just mixed the sugar into the strawberries when the phone rang, and she jumped in surprise. Rinsing her hands at the sink, she moved to the window to take a peek outside. Keith was nowhere in sight. The phone jangled a third time. No doubt he had an answering machine and it would pick up before long.

She'd just moved to the door when it opened, startling her again. He shot a quick glance at her as he hurried down the hall. The phone cut off in midring.

She heard the rumble of his voice as he spoke, could imagine that same soft sound murmuring in her ear. Whispering endearments, sweet promises.

Victor had whispered plenty in that year they were together, avowals of love, pledges of fealty. Commitment to her was never the problem. He would have never left her.

He would have been hers forever, if only she could stand to live in hell.

When Keith returned to the kitchen, his expression was stormy. Sara couldn't help the trill of fear that clamored inside her; it took a long deep breath to calm herself. Keith's gaze narrowed on her, and for a moment she fought the impulse to run. But it was just exasperation in his face, and she realized it had nothing to do with her.

"I'll bring her tomorrow," he said. "Take her back after. For the moment, that's all I can commit to."

Relief eased the knot inside her. She had tomorrow at least. "Thank you."

His mouth compressed into a tight line. "What happened before...we can't..." He looked away, then back at her. "It isn't you. I just don't—"

"I don't, either. I'm not interested in...relationships."

She'd piqued his curiosity. She could see the speculation in his eyes. But as much as he evidently had to hide, he wasn't asking. "Is the shortcake ready?"

She smiled, grateful for the change of subject. "It's cool enough, I think."

He pulled down a couple bowls and Sara served up the split biscuits and sugared strawberries. They ate standing in the kitchen at opposite ends of the island. He finished first, his gaze fixed on her as she spooned up mouthfuls of berries and delicate pastry. He might as well have been touching her.

She left as quickly as she could, thanking him for dinner, telling him she'd see him in the morning. As she drove away, she felt as wired as if she'd downed ten cups of espresso, each nerve ending sparking with energy. She read late into the night, her eyes burning, her thoughts chasing themselves. When she finally fell asleep, she dreamed of him, images of Keith woven in her dreams.

As the afternoon sun beat down on his pickup truck, Keith exited Interstate 80 and turned toward Hart Valley. It had been a hell of a day, starting with a nasty razor cut when he'd let his attention drift to Sara instead of the task at hand, then Linda Johnston's smug interest when he picked up Grace. After he'd dropped off the eight-year-old at Sara's, he'd had his showdown with his foreman, Wyatt, a follow-up to last night's rancorous phone call. He'd nearly lost Wyatt to a competing construction company, had had to make promises that were damn hard to make to keep the young foreman.

Promises that opened up possibilities Keith wasn't sure he was ready to explore. Wyatt was fed up with Keith's micromanaging of every job site. He wanted more autonomy, more responsibility. In short, he didn't want his boss looking over his shoulder on every project, wanted Keith to demonstrate his confidence in him.

Slowing as he drove through town, Keith let the ramifications of his agreement with Wyatt sink in. He hadn't taken time off from the business in at least five years, had convinced himself that weekends off were enough and besides, he couldn't risk being absent. But he'd just committed a solid two weeks' trial to Wyatt, giving him the opportunity to be in charge of their three current job sites. There wasn't anything keeping Keith from taking that time off.

He turned onto Stony Creek Road, considering his options. He figured he had at least three choices. Take off on a two-week vacation, maybe finally take that fishing trip up in Montana. He doubted he'd relax much so far from home, worrying over how the construction was coming along. He could stay home for the two weeks, get a few things done around the house. The biggest problem with that option was that it wouldn't keep him busy enough. He'd likely end up dropping in on Wyatt, just to see how things were going.

Option three would keep him plenty busy. He'd called Jameson himself, gotten a rundown on everything on the Rescued Hearts program's wish list. The barn, the wash rack, the addition to Sara's small house. Additional paddocks to allow them to bring in more horses in the summers. A covered patio for crafts and lunches.

So deep in thought, he missed the ranch's gravel driveway and had to pull into the nearest turnout to reverse. Then he had to wait for a white minivan to pull out before he could make his turn. Jeremy waved from the back seat as his mom drove away.

The other students were still in the arena, just climbing off their horses. A sixth horse, apparently Jeremy's, was untacked and camped out at the tie racks. Keith parked the truck, sat there a few minutes trying to wrap his mind around what he was contemplating. He couldn't get all the jobs done that Jameson wanted, but could make a good start. It wasn't the amount of work that was the sticking point.

Sara turned toward the truck as she walked from the

arena and lifted an arm in greeting. He pushed open the door, dropped from the cab. She'd already escorted the kids over to the tie racks by the time he started toward her and was too busy helping them untack to notice his approach.

Just watching her, in her shoulder-baring tank top and denim shorts, her hair escaping her ponytail, he burned to pull her into his arms. If he'd thought kissing her was a bad idea before he'd done the deed, he knew now it was a mistake monumental in proportions. The brief taste he'd had of her mouth had made it nearly impossible to think of anything besides tasting her again.

But if he were to offer what he had in mind, he'd have to completely quash even the slightest notion of kissing Sara again. Because he damn well wasn't going any further down that road than he already had.

He posted himself at one end of the tack room, keeping out of the way of the hubbub as the assistants helped the students put away saddles, blankets and bridles. Sara would lend a hand as needed, but generally she'd stand back to let the kids work out their problems with how to unbuckle a strap or where to put a saddle away. Part of the learning process, Keith supposed.

He felt her gaze on him a few times, caught her looking out of the corner of his eye. He kept his attention on the kids and the horses, not too keen on making that connection. Looking at her meant wanting her and he was going to do his damnedest to stop wanting her.

Finally her assistants untied the first four horses to lead them over to the paddocks. Grace stayed back with Dudley, leaning against the gelding's chestnut shoulder. The flea-specked gray dozed at the other end of the tie rack.

Sara moved toward him. "It'll be just a minute. Ryan and Dani will be back to take the last two horses."

"I can help you take them over."

Grace led Dudley while Sara remained at the gelding's head, fingers hooked in his halter. Keith led the gray pony on Dudley's other side, away from Grace. Walking beside Keith between the horses, Sara's shoulders were close enough that they nearly brushed his.

"How'd she do today?" Keith asked, pitching his voice low.

Sara shrugged. "About where we left off Friday."

The helpers had gotten their horses put away and were heading back down the hill. "Ryan, Dani," Sara called out, "could you help Grace put Dudley and Pearly away?"

The two teens did an about-face with the horses, Grace still clutching Dudley's lead rope. Sara waited until they were out of earshot. "I made some calls at lunch. I found a few people who can get her here or take her home. But they're complete strangers to Grace. I don't know how she'll react to that."

Up by the paddocks, the little girl patted Dudley's nose, saying her goodbyes. "How's the horse doing?" Keith asked.

"As lame as ever." There was an edgy tone to her words. "But doing his best for her."

Which Keith wasn't. A sense of guilt nibbled at him, despite the fact that Grace wasn't his responsibility at all. Still he couldn't deny he had the means to help her.

Grace had started back toward them, flanked by the two helpers. With a light touch on Sara's shoulder, Keith urged her back down toward the arena. "I want to talk something through with you."

She ducked his hand, but moved along with him down the hill. Below them, cars had started pulling in. "Let me get the other students off."

While she spoke to the arriving parents, Keith walked to the knoll where she'd mentioned she wanted the barn. He'd have to borrow the Bobcat again to grade a pad. They could just lay down road base for the foundation, but concrete would last longer and he'd already made arrangements with his cement guy.

The last car pulled away, leaving just his pickup and Dani's red car. Sara made her way up the hill toward him. Watching her approach, the rebellious auburn hair around her lightly tanned face, the strength in her long legs, her generous hips, only reminded him what he risked in her company. Not just the heat she incited in him, but something more that reached too deep inside him.

She breathed a little harder from the exertion of the climb. "Dani will keep an eye on Grace."

He wondered what her breath would feel like curling against his skin, then shut down that train of thought. "I spoke to Jameson."

Hope flickered in her eyes. "About Grace?"

"Not exactly." He couldn't seem to get the words out, knowing what he would be committing himself to. "I've agreed to do some more work. The barn and the wash rack."

"What about your business?" She crossed her arms over her middle, framing her breasts.

He dragged his gaze to her face. "I'm on vacation."

"Then, Grace—"

He wished his conscience could let him walk away. No such luck. "I can bring her."

The smile that lit Sara's face set off an ache inside him, forcing him to look away. He squelched the rawness until it became bearable. "Draw up what you want for the barn," he told her with only the barest roughness to his voice. "And whatever else you want built. I'll get done what I can these two weeks."

She squeezed his hand. "Thank you. Thank you so much."

He nodded brusquely, then started down the hill. He had to get Grace to her sitter's, had to go check prices on pipe panels for the barn and plumbing supplies to run water to the wash rack. Good excuses to avoid the real truth—if he didn't leave her now, he'd be holding her again. And in that moment, he'd have a damn hard time letting her go.

Thursday at noon, Sara relaxed in the coolness of her small kitchen, enjoying her few moments of lunchtime peace. As she took a last bite of her sandwich, she scanned the student status reports spread out on the dinette table. She'd completed everyone's except Grace's, although the eight-year-old's was nearly finished. She would add a few more notes to all of them tomorrow to have them ready when the parents arrived.

Keith had been in and out today after dropping off

Grace, bringing supplies, unloading them, then taking off again. He had the pad dug for the barn, and had framed it for the concrete foundation. The concrete would be delivered sometime next week, so he'd busied himself with getting the wash rack ready for the pour, as well.

She heard the rumble of a diesel engine and peered out the kitchen window. Keith pulled in, his truck kicking up dust in the noontime heat. Sara had managed to steer clear of him, busying herself with the students, finding plenty to do in the house in the afternoons if he returned after dropping off Grace.

More than once, she'd been tempted to bring him out iced tea or lemonade, just to talk with him, spend some time with him. But she couldn't be near him without wanting him to kiss her again. And she couldn't let that happen.

Sara checked her watch. She had another twenty minutes of lunchtime before the session started up again. Out in the noon heat, the students and helpers ate their bag lunches in the shade of a massive oak.

She could keep an eye on them through the kitchen window, see Jeremy running circles around the picnic table Sara had set up under the tree, Marisa talking the ears off anyone who would listen. Grace sat in her habitual silence next to Dani.

Setting her plate by the sink, Sara unearthed a pair of scissors from the kitchen junk drawer. The classified section still lay open on the table next to the portable phone and she quickly found the "horse for sale" ad she'd circled. Clipping around the ad, she set it next to the directions she'd scribbled on a notepad.

After enduring four straight days of horse camp, Dudley's lameness had only gotten worse. Last night, she'd called Dr. Fox, the large animal vet who volunteered his time and expertise in caring for the program's horses. He'd been out to see Dudley more than once and after she'd updated the vet, his diagnosis was the same as it had been on his last visit—ringbone. The poor old guy was hurting and he wouldn't be getting any better.

Sara had given him plenty of bute today to ease his pain and would tomorrow, as well, but after that he would be officially retired. The old gelding could hang out in the pasture here for a while, but his long-term home would be Tom Jarret's ranch on the other side of town.

After camp ended tomorrow she planned to look at a new horse for the program. It would be best to take a truck and trailer down to bring the horse back if the mare was a good fit, but Sara had never hauled before, not even during her summer at the dude ranch. The two-horse slant load Tom had offered to lend her wouldn't be the best initiation into trailering, especially taking the narrow curves of Highway 49 with such a wide rig.

Tom was tied up and couldn't drive himself. He told her Keith had plenty of experience hauling heavy equipment around and would likely have no trouble driving a horse trailer. Tom figured it was worth asking Keith if he could help.

Turning to check on the group at the picnic table, she saw Keith walking over from the parking area. Her reaction to his approach told her exactly why driving with him tomorrow would be perilous. But with such short notice, she likely had no other choice.

As Keith neared the house, Grace slipped from the bench to run toward him. He waited for her, bending as she threw her arms around him. He looked uncomfortable folding his tall body down to Grace's height, but he didn't let go until the little girl did. He watched her as she returned to the table, then continued toward Sara's front door.

She had the door open so quickly after his first knock, he stepped back in surprise. "I saw you from the window." It struck her he might think she was looking for him. "I was monitoring the kids."

"Sorry to interrupt your lunch."

"I have to get the afternoon session started anyway."

He stared at her, his gaze intent. His blue eyes pulled at her, inviting her to move closer.

An invitation she wasn't about to accept. She made a show of checking her watch. "What was it you wanted?"

He must have realized he was staring. He looked away. "The concrete truck will be here on Monday. Before camp starts."

"Great. Thanks."

She waited for him to move, so she could get past him. But even two feet away, she imagined she felt his heat.

Over at the picnic bench, Dani and Ryan were supervising lunch cleanup, directing the students to gather up their trash and carry it to the cans by the tack room. As Grace walked by, she offered the faintest wisp of a smile for Keith.

"I found a horse to replace Dudley. Down in Sutter Creek."

Keith watched Grace, standing alone by a tie post. "How's she going to handle giving him up?"

"Not well." Putting aside her worries about Grace for the moment, she zeroed in on her more immediate concern. "Have you ever hauled horses?"

His gaze narrowed on her. "A few times."

"Think you can handle a two-horse slant?"

He hesitated before answering. "Sure."

She took a breath. "Then I need your help tomorrow."

Friday afternoon, Sara threw water bottles, apples and granola bars into a canvas tote, grabbed the directions and locked up the house. Stopping to filch a bag of horse treats and her helmet from the tack room, she carried everything out to the parking area to wait for Keith.

On his way back from taking Grace to the sitter, he'd be stopping by the Double J Ranch to pick up Tom Jarret's rig. Anticipation of the trip ahead held her in its grip. Despite her trepidation at the long drive in close quarters of the Jarret pickup, she couldn't deny the sizzle of excitement inside her.

She had to school herself to think of him as just another man, a friendly neighbor like Jameson O'Connell or Tom Jarret. Except he wasn't particularly friendly and the feelings Keith roused in her were nothing like the cautious affection she felt for Jameson and Tom. Those two happily married men never sent off even a scintilla of interest in her, both of them too enthralled with their wives, Nina and Andrea.

Precisely what Keith felt for her, she had no idea. The

heat of his gaze, the few lingering touches that got past her barrier of fear, those two incredible, incomprehensible kisses—what did it all mean? Even more important, what did she want it to mean? She didn't want him any closer…did she? She didn't want to be involved with him at all.

At least that was what she told herself. But when she remembered how his mouth had felt against hers, his warmth seeping into her, the rawness of his breathing stroking her nerves, it was hard to keep to that resolve. Even reminding herself about Victor and the disaster he'd turned out to be didn't seem to keep her heart from racing when she imagined Keith's touch.

How *had* it been with Victor when she'd first met him? She was in her first year of grad school, starting her masters in counseling degree. Between her personal history and her specialization in marriage, family and child counseling, she should have been well educated in recognizing an abuser.

But Victor flew right under her radar. Maybe it had been her preoccupation with school, or the worry that Ashley wouldn't get her scholarships her second year at Berkeley. She'd been struggling to come up with that month's rent, as well, and in fact met Victor in the laundry room as she counted out her last quarters for the washer. He gave her a handful of change to augment her limited stash, coming across as a kind, gentle man.

The first time he kissed her, he'd gone so slow, she had nothing to fear. There wasn't much in the way of sparks; it had been pleasant enough, but not earth-shattering.

When he'd gone a little further the next time, his tongue had felt foreign in her mouth, but she put it down to her own mental blocks.

But Keith's kiss—sparks didn't even begin to describe the sensations. And to her shame she wanted desperately to have him taste her, wanted more than just his mouth on hers.

The whine of a laboring diesel engine dragged her from the past and she looked up to see a truck and trailer slowly turn into the gravel drive. She stayed where she was by the arena as Keith expertly circled the parking area, positioning the pickup and two-horse slant to exit again. She started toward him, waving him back in the truck as he was about to step down.

Trotting alongside the long trailer, she resolved to banish Victor and past mistakes from her mind today. She'd focus firmly on the present—the horse she'd be seeing this afternoon and whether it was suitable for the program.

But as she sat next to Keith in the cab of the Double J truck, she realized the present was even more dangerous than the past. The present included feelings she didn't understand for a man she didn't really know. Keeping him from her mind had already proved nearly impossible.

Chapter Eight

Driving east on State Highway 16, Keith eased the Double J truck over to the right and made the turn onto Highway 49. Beside him, Sara stared out the window, scrunched about as far as she could be to her side of the cab.

Their conversation had been pretty limited so far, his focus on navigating the rig through Sacramento rush hour traffic, hers on whatever she found so fascinating out the window. He supposed it was just as well she kept to herself over in that right bucket seat. Less of a distraction.

Even still, the silence was just about driving him crazy. Slowing for the twists of Highway 49, he shot her a quick glance. "What's the turn once we get into Sutter Creek?"

She referred to her sheet of directions. "Left on Sutter Hill, then right on Ridge Road."

The names sparked dim memories. "I camped near here as a kid." He hadn't thought about it in years.

She scanned the passing terrain. "It's beautiful country."

Lower in elevation, live and black oak dotted the rolling hillsides rather than the pines and cedars they were accustomed to in Hart Valley. The scent of campfire smoke, the taste of trout caught in a rushing snow-fed creek resurfaced from some corner of his brain.

Recall of the past set off a habitual ache inside him. He blanked the images from his mind, slowing to a crawl as he drove through Dry Town and Amador City. The towns were so small you'd miss them if you sneezed, nothing more than a small collection of antique shops and bed-and-breakfasts.

Amador City behind them, he pulled into the right lane to let the cars behind him pass. Only a couple more miles to Sutter Creek.

By the time they reached the town limits it was nearly six and his stomach rumbled with hunger. "I'll take one of those apples now."

As she bent to retrieve the canvas tote, Highway 49 narrowed into a two-lane splitting Sutter Creek. They crept along between parked cars on the right and oncoming traffic on the left.

As he stopped to make the turn onto Sutter Hill, he glanced over at her. Golden delicious in her hand, cheeks flushed, she straightened and turned toward him. Her auburn hair, as always, beguiled him. Rebelliously mussed, strands of rich wine curled softly around her face.

A horn blasted and he realized oncoming traffic had cleared and he could make his turn. Ignoring the proffered apple for the moment, he swung the truck and trailer left onto Sutter Hill.

"Sorry," she said, sounding breathless.

He could all too easily imagine what activity might steal her breath. He shook off the vivid picture. "Not your fault."

After the short jog to Ridge Road, they hit a straightaway and he held out his hand for the apple. As she dropped the fruit in his palm, he resisted the impulse to stroke her wrist. With nearly two tons of horse trailer behind him, he had no business letting his attention stray.

She'd taken an apple out for herself and she passed it back and forth from hand to hand before finally taking a bite. "Did you camp with your parents?"

He quashed a dull throb of pain. "My dad."

Her smile jolted him off-track so he was unprepared for her next question. "Your mom didn't like camping?"

His pain became bitterness. "She was gone by then."

Her smile faded, replaced by sympathy. "My mom died when I was eight."

He ought to just leave it at that. It was ancient history; what did it matter if Sara assumed *gone* meant *dead?*

But the lie of omission didn't sit right. "My mother walked out when I was six."

"Oh." The soft spoken word might have eased some of his hurt, but he'd learned not to count on healing. "Where is she now?" Sara asked.

"Dead. Cancer. More than twenty years ago."

"Did you ever—"

"No. I never saw her again."

He'd told himself for years he didn't care about the loose ends his mother's abandonment had left untied, that he never got answers for the thousands of questions her departure had generated. But late at night, particularly in those long dark hours when he couldn't banish Christopher's face from his mind's eye, he didn't believe his own assurances.

He caught a glimpse of a sign reading Sandinsky on a narrow gravel road just as he sailed right past it. Sara turned in her seat. "I think that was it."

He had to continue close to a mile down Ridge Road before he found a turnout big enough to turn the rig around. After pulling off the road, he took a last bite of the apple, then looked for a place to set the core.

Sara plucked it from his hand. "I'll take it."

His palm was still sticky with juice. A fantasy hit with sudden clarity—Sara licking the tart sweetness from his skin, then tracing up his arm with the tip of her tongue. "You have a napkin?" he asked, his voice hoarse.

Her gaze fixed on him and he almost wondered if she could read his mind. Something had brought that color to her cheeks.

She dug a napkin out of the bag and wet it from the water bottle. If she made a move to clean his hand, he was damn well getting out of the truck.

But she just passed him the napkin and he swiped it across his hand. Checking for traffic, he pulled back onto the pavement toward the gravel road. He kept his attention on his driving as she tidied up herself.

She took a drink from the water bottle. "Did your brothers or sisters go camping with you?"

"My half brother and sister were too young. By the time they were old enough to go with us, I'd lost interest." Around the time he'd heard his mother had died. Without ever coming back home, without ever seeing him again.

But until then, camping had been the one bright spot in a painful childhood. His stepmother, Regina, had done her best to mother him. Even when his new siblings Michael and Janna came along, Regina made a point to include him in everything. If her love for the two younger kids was any stronger than what she felt for Keith, she never showed it.

But by the time Regina married his father, Keith just didn't have it in him to accept her affection. He'd already wasted his emotions on his mother and there just wasn't any more to give.

He spotted the gravel driveway in time and turned slowly onto the narrow track. "How far down?"

"A mile. There's a wrought-iron gate."

A few minutes later he pulled up to a battered farmhouse surrounded by pasture. Cattle and horses grazed together on the irrigated grass. A small black mare stood alone in a round pen, dozing in the sunshine.

He figured she'd hop out before he even killed the engine. But she lingered in her seat, even as an old cowboy with a hitch in his get-along approached the truck.

The light touch of her fingers on the back of his hand sent a jolt up his arm. The earnest sympathy in her face nearly undid him. "I never got to say goodbye, either."

* * *

Stepping from the truck, Sara greeted old Bob Sandinsky, then glanced back inside the cab. Keith sat stock-still, staring out at the acres of green pasture. If what she'd said had hurt or helped, she'd never know looking at his face. But she suspected she'd crossed over a line she never should have.

Putting aside the puzzle of Keith for the moment, she walked over toward the round pen with the old cowboy. "Tell me about her," Sara said, gesturing toward the dozing mare.

"She's twenty-eight years old," Bob said. "A mustang from the northern Nevada range." He turned toward the house and hollered, "Elizabeth!"

A twelve-year-old girl came running, slamming the door on her way out of the house. "Go fetch a saddle and bridle for Luna," the cowboy told the girl.

Elizabeth cast a suspicious look Sara's way, no doubt reluctant to let go of a favorite horse. Sara smiled at her, but the towhead just scowled.

She heard the truck door slam and watched Keith head toward the small shed where Elizabeth struggled under the weight of a heavy leather saddle. He spoke to her, gesturing once toward Sara. Sara didn't know what he said, but the girl handed over the saddle and by the time she'd reached the round pen, she was smiling.

Elizabeth unlatched the round pen gate and walked toward the mare with the halter and lead rope. Keith set the saddle on the rail. "Hard to let go, I guess."

Sara had let go of so many things in her life, it had become second nature. Learning how to hold on, that was the challenge.

Elizabeth led the mare over toward Sara. "Luna's a great little pony. Just too worn-out to chase cows anymore."

The girl tacked up the black mustang and climbed on, showing off a bit with spins, side passes and a rollback. When Sara took her turn in the saddle, the mare calmly did everything asked of her. Even when Sara yelled and clapped loudly as she trotted around the ring, Luna didn't do anything more than twitch an ear.

Sara slid from the saddle and handed the reins over to Elizabeth. Stepping from the round pen, she gestured to Keith and he walked with her out of earshot of Bob and Elizabeth.

"What do you think?" Sara asked.

He shrugged. "Not my decision."

"I realize that. But I'd like your opinion."

He stared down at her. "You know she's a damn good horse. You don't need me to tell you."

She didn't. But she thought if she could get him talking about the horse, maybe it would smooth over the sharp edges that stood between them. Besides, now that she had to decide, she wasn't the least bit sure anymore.

Sara glanced over at the round pen where Elizabeth had untacked Luna and stood with her arm draped over the black mare's withers. "She'd be the first horse I've authorized for the program. The others were already at the ranch when I started."

"Is she what you need?"

Somehow, coming from him, the question seemed provocative, as if he was asking about something entirely different. "She was stocked up in her hind legs."

"Old horses get that way."

"It could be from an injury." She knew she was playing devil's advocate, but she wanted his reassurance.

"The swelling went down after you worked her."

As Elizabeth led Luna back to pasture, Sara scrutinized every movement the mare made. "What if she comes up lame a week after I buy her?"

She felt his touch on her cheek as he turned her toward him. "Is she what you need?"

Every thought fled her brain. Except for the feel of his hand on her face, the brilliant blue of his eyes. Bob had gone into the house and his granddaughter was turning the mare out with the other horses. Neither would see them if Keith leaned over to kiss her.

But he dropped his hand and her mind kick-started again. "She's exactly right. As long as she's sound."

As they headed toward the house, Bob emerged. His granddaughter stood by the pasture gate as if she couldn't bear to hear Sara's decision.

Sara climbed the steps while Keith waited below. "I'd like a vet to look her over, if you don't mind."

The old cowboy scuffed his boot on a battered porch step. "Twenty-eight years old, she's not gonna be perfect."

"I don't expect perfect."

"Too late for the vet tonight." Bob nodded over at the sun, low on the horizon.

Of course it was. "I guess we'll have to go home and come back tomorrow."

The old cowboy propped his hands on his skinny hips. "I got someone else seeing that horse in the morning."

"I can't take her until the vet sees her."

"Then we got a problem." Old Bob seemed to chew over the situation. "You folks could stay the night in town."

Stay overnight…with Keith? She couldn't help herself; she looked down at him waiting at the foot of the steps. He looked as stunned as her at Bob's suggestion, then something flickered in his face as if he considered the notion.

Keith ascended the steps until his tall frame was level with Bob's slight figure. "You know a vet we could call tonight to set things up for tomorrow?"

Bob rubbed his whisker-stubbled chin. "Doc Barton likely could come out."

Keith's gaze met Sara's. With those blue eyes on her, she would be crazy to say yes. But the black mustang was too nice a horse to pass up.

She cleared her throat. "I'd appreciate Dr. Barton's phone number."

The old cowboy disappeared inside, leaving Sara alone on the porch with Keith. Feeling a need for protection, she crossed her arms over her middle. "Can you stay the night?"

"Nothing I need to be back for."

"I'll pay for your room."

"No."

"Jameson will probably reimburse me."

He shook his head. "I pay my own way."

Bob emerged with a scrap of paper. "The phone number underneath Doc Barton's is the Blue Oak Inn. I hear their honeymoon suite is mighty nice."

Keith snatched the paper from him and handed it to Sara. She went back to the truck for her cell phone. She reached the vet's answering service and upon explaining the situation, she got a quick call back from Dr. Barton. After arranging things with the vet, she called Tom Jarret to make sure he could do without his truck and trailer until tomorrow.

She returned to the porch, edging around the smoldering Keith. "The vet can come at nine," she told Bob. "Will that work for you?"

"Sure thing." Tromping to the end of the porch, he yelled out, "Elizabeth! Get yourself in here for dinner." Then he stomped off into the house.

It was nearly eight and dusk had faded into near darkness. They headed back to the truck, Keith circling the rig carefully out of the driveway. Tension crackled in the air, leaving Sara breathless and sensitized.

"What first?" he asked. "Room or dinner?"

In the intimate dimness of the truck cab, the innocent question spilled over with possibilities. "Room first, then dinner."

Holding up the slip Bob had given her, she dialed the number for the inn. Fumbling for her credit card, she dropped it and had to grope for it on the floor. Her voice cracked as she read out the number.

Once they'd returned to town, Sara directed Keith to the Blue Oak and they pulled around back to park the rig. He killed the engine and they sat for a moment in the dark.

They were here on program business and would be renting separate rooms, but their being at the inn without so much as a single piece of luggage seemed a bit illicit. "I don't even have a toothbrush," Sara said, focusing on the necessities.

"There's one of those big box stores up the road," he told her. "Go on and check us in. I'll unhitch the trailer and we can drive the truck over there for a few things."

She opened the door, slid down to the pavement. Keith's intent blue eyes fixed on her, his face patterned with shadows in the dimness of the dome light. Her nerve endings prickled, the weight of his gaze palpable. She wanted nothing more than to climb back into the truck and into his arms.

He leaned toward her, and for an instant she thought he might take her hand, pull her inside. But he just said, "Meet you out front," before straightening.

Sara shut the door, cutting off the rampant images, and headed for the inn.

The jack on the trailer didn't want to budge at first and it gave Keith something to throw his energy into besides fantasizing about Sara. Once the crank got moving, he wrenched it around and around, lifting the tongue of the trailer higher to pop it off the ball of the truck hitch. The brute force work didn't take much mental capacity, but if he focused on the feel of the handle in his grip, the turns of the jack, he could hold off the forbidden.

Before long he had the trailer unhitched and secured with chocks and was back in the truck. As he drove around to the front of the inn, he saw her waiting on the porch. Tote bag clutched in her arms, she started toward him. She levered herself up into the truck.

Her voice was low over the rumble of the engine. "Do you want to eat first?"

With the mess of snakes in his stomach, he didn't think he could eat. "Let's get the shopping done."

He continued through town, Highway 49 now shrouded in darkness. His recall of the area surprised him. He hadn't been down this way in years, most recently when he'd taken a weekend fishing trip in a vain attempt at relaxation. He supposed he'd had some notion of recapturing the fleeting pleasures of his childhood, but soon discovered happiness was the most perishable of commodities.

He pulled into the store's nearly deserted parking lot and they went inside, splitting up. He wasn't about to skulk around the women's department with Sara while she picked out who knew what unmentionables. It was enough of a challenge keeping his mind on the up and up instead of the lurid fantasies it kept trying to visit.

She met up with him over by the toothpaste, a wadded up T-shirt under her arm. He could just imagine what she'd concealed inside that mint-green bundle.

They reached for the same brand of toothbrush, his fingers grazing hers. He jumped back to give her clearance, then made the mistake of looking over at a nearby display. Condoms filled the top three shelves, colorful boxes with names that conjured up a two-hour movie's worth of mental pictures. All of them staring at him and Sara.

Waiting for her to finish her selection, he grabbed what

he needed, then they made their way toward the checkout stand. T-shirt and shorts in one hand, toothbrush and paste in the other, he waited as Sara set down her items.

The checker grabbed the pale green T-shirt and a rose-pink bra and matching pair of undies tumbled onto the counter. Keith's hands gripped the packaging for the toothbrush tighter. He shouldn't even be looking at that little scrap of pink knit, but his brain had other ideas, keeping him riveted on Sara's intimate apparel.

After ringing up the T-shirt, the checker ran the panties over the scanner. She tried once, twice, but still the price wouldn't come up on the register. Waving the panties like a surrender flag, the checker yelled out, "Price check!"

He finally dragged his gaze away from Sara's underwear, and over at her. Her hands over her cheeks, she looked up at him. He expected the jolt of excitement—he couldn't seem to so much as glance at her without feeling it—but the sudden spurt of joy inside caught him off guard. He could see she was damned embarrassed, but humor lit her hazel eyes and he was pretty sure she was smiling.

Then she dropped her hands and laughed, the sound so appealing and infectious he couldn't hold back his own laughter. Before long, they were both doubled over, gasping for breath. Every time they looked up at each other, the laughter started all over again, Sara's soft hand on his arm for support. The clerk and manager must have thought they were downright insane.

Finally they'd paid for their purchases and escaped from the store. As they made their way back to the truck, it seemed as if for the moment the perennial weight that hung on Keith's shoulders had lifted. His heart hadn't felt so light in years.

Their bags tossed behind the seat, they belted themselves in and Keith reached for the key. He wasn't sure what made him look her way; it just seemed the constant link between them demanded it. And of course, he wasn't satisfied with just a look, not when he saw her eyes still moist from tears of laughter, her mouth still curved in a smile.

He released the latch on the seat belt without thinking, sliding across the console toward her. Cradling her head with one hand, he tugged her toward him, covering her mouth with his. Her hands on his chest tensed as if she was ready to push him away. He would have let her go in a heartbeat, but then her fingers relaxed, curled against the knit of his T-shirt.

He wanted to dive inside her mouth, wanted to touch her everywhere. He drew the tip of his tongue across the seam of her lips, the taste of her driving him wild. She didn't pull away, but she didn't immediately open to him, either, and it was obvious she wasn't too sure she wanted things going any further.

He thought his heart would pound out of his chest, but he started to back away. She grabbed his T-shirt, keeping him right there. "Just a kiss," she gasped out. "Just one."

There wasn't any way in hell he could deny her.

Chapter Nine

With Keith's hands on her, his mouth on her, Sara was terrified and out of her mind with sensation all at once. She knew she should have let him pull away when he offered, but her need spoke for her, whispering an invitation, nearly begging for his touch.

What could one kiss hurt? A real kiss, his tongue in her mouth, just a little bit of Keith inside her heart. She needed that small fragment of him, to soothe the constant loneliness of her soul, the persistent fear that chased her like a wraith.

This time when his tongue trailed across her mouth, she opened to him, letting out a sigh of pleasure as he slipped it inside. He didn't immediately plunge deep as Victor had always done. Instead Keith took his time with gentle, sipping kisses, tender forays into her mouth that drove a moan from her throat.

Fumbling for the latch of the seat belt, she released it, edging even closer to him. Shifting, he pulled her into his lap, moving into her seat at the same time. She felt the hard ridge of him against her leg, fought the shocking impulse to put her hand there. Instead she hooked it around his neck, holding him as close as she could.

Now he dived inside with his tongue, but still gently, leisurely, as if he had all the time in the world. The tension in his arms around her told another story, of passion held in check. That he could control that heat, temper his urges instead of overpowering her with his lust was a revelation. That crumbled another wall inside her, leaving her that much more exposed.

The realization intensified her own arousal and she felt as if she'd burst out of her skin. When he tugged her tank top from the waistband of her jeans, a trill of fear sounded briefly inside her, but the touch of his fingers against her bare skin washed it away.

He drew lazy circles along her side, each one looping higher. An old memory intruded—Victor's hand squeezing her breast, not quite painful, but never pleasant, either. If Keith did the same, if he closed his hand too tightly over that tender flesh—

Instead he stroked her softly, and a moan emerged from deep inside her. It was just his thumb trailing along the underside of her breast, the slightest pressure through the satin of her bra. But honeyed heat spread from that contact point, streaking her body with sensation. Her heart pounded so loudly in her ears, her world seemed to vibrate in response.

With the first brush of his thumb over her nipple, her head fell back, her body felt weak and energized all at once. His mouth moved along her throat, and he kissed her, tasted her, leaving fire in his wake.

It was impossible to sit still. She squirmed, pressing her hip against his hard ridge, and she heard the breath go out of him. He sat motionless, his body rigid with tension. Air made its ragged way into his lungs, and as his chest heaved, it pressed against her breast, sensitive and aching for his touch.

"Two choices here," he rasped out. "Go back to the inn and finish this. Or stop it now."

With that slap of reality, he might as well have dashed cold water over her. She felt the heat of embarrassment rise in her face and she levered carefully off his lap. Head turned away so she didn't have to look at him, she waited for him to return to his side before taking her seat again, pulling the seat belt across her with a shaky hand.

She struggled for breath to speak. "We'd better get back."

His hand missed the key the first time he reached for it. "What about dinner?" The engine roared as he started it.

Just the thought of eating tightened her stomach. "Can we pick up fast food? I'd rather just eat in my room."

She shot him a sidelong glance. He sat so stiffly, he could have been carved out of granite. Not the chill stone of winter, but summer heated rock that could warm you to the core.

She tried to obliterate the last few minutes from her mind as he pulled out of the parking lot and made his way back to Highway 49. At the burger joint drive-through, she only had to relay her order to him, then she could sink back into her mortified silence.

At the inn, they climbed the stairs together, each of them clutching their bag of purchases and a paper sack of deep-fried dinner. He insisted on walking her to her room before he took the stairs to his on the third floor.

Digging in her purse for the room key, she dropped the paper sack. With a huff of impatience, he took the plastic bag from her, then bent to pick up the grease-stained sack.

When she pushed open the door, he followed her in, setting his burdens down on a small round table just inside the room. She dropped her tote bag on the bed, keeping its width between them.

The longing to run to him, to feel his arms around her again surged inside her. She thought her heart might explode from her chest. His rugged face, those intense blue eyes, the tenderness of his kiss—she wanted it all again.

But she stayed right where she was, even as he stood immobile over by the door. She should ask him to leave, tell him how tired she was, that she wanted nothing more than to fall into bed. But truly, if she climbed under those covers, she wanted him with her, his strong body stretched alongside hers, every inch of him in contact with her skin.

He took a step, just one, and she thought he might move toward her. But then he turned away, toward the door. As he retreated, her heart ached with the loss.

He'd nearly closed it behind him when he pushed it

open again. Hand gripping the doorknob as if to keep him anchored, he locked his gaze with hers, his expression fierce.

"You asked," he said.

Her cheeks warmed again. "I know."

"Don't ask again." The words were clipped. "Please."

Then he shut the door, the sound jolting her. Still standing behind the protection of the bed, she looked around at the pretty, frilly room, with its cheerful cabbage rose wallpaper and shelves crowded with bric-a-brac. To the depths of her soul, she wanted to call him back.

Perfectly safe now, she crossed the room to the table where Keith had left her things and dumped the fast food in the trash.

Sara muddled through the next day—the awkward breakfast at the inn with Keith sitting stiffly on the other side of the table, the stifling silence as they drove back to the ranch, her awareness of him overwhelming her senses.

At least during the vet check, she had the doctor's exam of the mustang mare to distract her, could keep her attention on signs of lameness and blood tests. Keith stayed by the truck, pacing its length, back and forth, even edgier than her. When she made the mistake of looking over at him once or twice, she thought she'd melt under the heat of his gaze and it took an effort to bring her mind back to what the vet was telling her.

The mare passed with flying colors, the stiffness in her left front leg working out easily with exercise, her vitals all normal for an older horse. The vet gave her a rundown of suggested supplements to keep the geriatric mare in good condition, the same products she already used on most of her horses. She wrote a check from the Rescued Hearts account for both the vet and seller, then led the horse around to the back of the trailer.

Keith had it open and ready and he stood by the door. "Need any help?"

She concentrated on the mare, now a bit skittish at the prospect of going into a strange trailer. "I'll let you know."

The horse stood between them, sniffing the trailer floor. While Sara let the mare's nerves settle, it seemed the most natural thing to let her gaze stray to Keith over by the right rear door. His face seemed etched with the same tiredness she felt after her sleepless night.

When the mare put a foot up into the trailer, Sara wasn't quite ready and had to jump to keep up. Now that she'd given the trailer her seal of approval, the mare stepped right up to the trailer tie, then looked back at Sara as if wondering what the hold up was. Sara quickly clipped the horse in place, closed the slant divider, then exited the trailer. She and Keith closed the back doors, side by side.

That spot of privacy behind the trailer was a temptation, whispering to Sara to lift her hands to his chest, slide them up to his shoulders, to pull him down. Keith leaned toward her, just an inch, then he straightened. Stepping past her, he headed for the cab of the truck.

They allowed Elizabeth one last goodbye before pulling out. Sara had given the girl the address and phone number of Rescued Hearts, inviting her to visit anytime. That seemed to soothe the girl's tears.

The drive back to Hart Valley seemed to stretch endlessly, not so much because the extra weight of the horse made for slower going, but because of the pin drop silence in the truck. A million scattered thoughts whirled in Sara's mind, but every time she'd frame even the most innocuous sentence, one glance at Keith silenced her. Even the simplest words, when exchanged with Keith, seemed intimate and erotic.

The mare was a good traveler and they made it back to the NJN Ranch without incident. She whinnied at the other horses when Sara led her out, then when Sara put her in the covered arena, she galloped around, tail flying.

By the time she returned to the rig, Keith was already in the truck, engine rumbling. He opened the window. "I'll clean up the trailer at Tom's."

"It's nearly lunchtime. Would you like to—"

"No. That's not a good idea."

"Thanks so much for your help." The rote courtesy didn't come close to expressing the maelstrom she felt inside. "I'll see you Monday."

He put the truck in gear and slowly turned toward the driveway. Sara longed to call him back even knowing the road that would lead her down.

She stood there until she couldn't hear the engine anymore, until the dust the rig had kicked up settled, until the baffling throb of pain inside her eased. Then she damped her thoughts of Keith and turned her focus back on the horses.

The week of camp seemed to crawl by, as if Sara had to physically slog through the tension between her and

Keith each day. He kept conversation with her to a minimum, their discussion of matters relating to Grace or the building of the barn as brief as possible. The few times she let herself look up the hill where he worked, he was mercifully busy with his labors.

Most days, he brought a young man to help, Brandon Walker, the sheriff deputy's son. The young teen provided a buffer between her and Keith, made the perfect excuse for avoiding anything personal between them. It was just as well, since privacy would only lead to another error in judgment on her part.

By Thursday, she had plenty to distract her anyway. Although she'd been able to persuade Grace to ride Pearly instead of Dudley, putting one of the more experienced students on the new mare, Grace shut down more and more as her third week of camp came to a close. Sara had already floated the proposition to Jameson that he sponsor Grace another week, but she hadn't quite been able to answer his pointed question—will it help her? It seemed the little girl was content to float along in a kind of stasis, the horses insulating her from fully facing the demons inside her.

The day's session over, the other students fetched by their parents, only Grace remained. Sara had even sent Dani home, since the teen had worked far above and beyond these past few weeks, and Gabe and Lori Walker had picked up Brandon an hour ago on their way to the Bay Area for a San Francisco Giants game.

Keith was just finishing laying rubber mats on the concrete floors of the barn stalls. He didn't have all the siding on the exterior walls yet, but the roof was on and all the gates hung.

Grace had been helping Sara tidy the tack room, a never-ending job. Taking a peek out the window, Sara could see Keith gathering equipment and shutting toolboxes. She supposed now was as good a time as ever to talk to him. The worst he could do was say no.

She put out a hand to Grace. "Let's go up and visit Keith, sweetheart."

Grace took her hand with a shy smile. That at least was some progress. She still didn't make a sound, but the little girl would let a smile slip out once in a while, taking the edge off her constant solemnity.

After the dimness of the tack room, the late-afternoon sun blinded her a moment and she had to dip her head to shield her eyes from the brilliance. She wasn't halfway up the hill before Grace let go, and when Sara shaded her eyes from the bright sunshine, she saw Keith had come down to meet them. He carried a toolbox in one hand and a wound-up extension cord hung on his shoulder, but he dropped to one knee to give Grace a hug.

Sara stopped a few feet away from them. "Can we help you bring anything down?"

He straightened, his shadowed face backlit by the sun. "I left my water bottle. Everything else can stay until tomorrow."

About to ask Grace to retrieve the bottle, the little girl surprised Sara when she trotted up the hill on her own volition. That gave Sara only a few seconds of time alone with Keith.

"There's going to be a picnic on Saturday, at the Marbleville County Park," she said quickly. "For all the camp kids from the past three weeks, and their parents. I'd like you to come."

He wanted to say no, she could see that much in his face. But he glanced over at Grace as she walked carefully down the hill, her thin arms wrapped around the large plastic bottle. "Grace is going?"

"And Alicia." Sara angled her body so she could see him more clearly. "Is that a problem?"

"No." He sighed heavily. "I'll think about it. Let you know."

"Okay. Thanks."

They continued down the hill together, walking toward Keith's truck. Sara tried to relieve Grace of the water bottle, but she refused to relinquish it. Since it was nearly empty and light enough for the little girl to carry, Sara gave up the battle.

Keith helped Grace into the truck, but before he could climb in himself, Sara stopped him. "I've been trying to work out a way to talk to you about this…"

"The picnic?" He knew he was being obtuse, she could see it in his eyes.

"Friday night. That kiss."

His gaze drilled into her. "That was a hell of a lot more than a kiss."

Warmth melted inside her at the memory. "It was a mistake."

His face set, he swung into the truck and cranked the engine. "I have to get Grace to day care."

The window went up as he backed the truck, pulling out in a cloud of dust. A faint breeze teased the floating particles, sending them off toward the lower pasture. She wished she could float away with them, just grab hold and let the breeze lift her, too. Disappear from the world as she'd always yearned to as a child.

But her world was far different than the one she'd suffered through for seven years after her mother's death. She had work she loved now, friends around her, a myriad of people who cared about her. The busybodies of Hart Valley might exasperate her at times, with their interest in every detail of her life, but she loved them nonetheless.

The dust had dispersed and quiet had settled on the ranch. The sun had crawled closer to the horizon of treetops and the temperature had eased, signaling a cool evening. Maybe she could keep her window open tonight.

As she stepped into the kitchen, her gaze strayed to her address book and the folded scrap of newspaper that didn't quite fit inside. She'd dug the paper out of the trash, had torn out the crumpled photo from the stock car race. Now she tugged it free, stared down at the man in the crowd shot who couldn't possibly be her father…

Smoothing the rumpled scrap of newspaper on the counter, Sara tried again to discern the features of that familiar, frightening face. The photographer had focused on the wreckage in the foreground, not on the crowd beyond it. The faces weren't distinct enough to be certain.

But it could be him! her unreasoning fear shouted.

She shut her eyes, covering her face with her hands as a familiar impulse to run welled up inside her. She'd done it for so many years—escape. But how could she leave everyone in the lurch—Grace, her other students, Jameson…Keith?

The guilt at leaving the children cut sharply enough. The thought of never seeing Keith again made her knees buckle and she had to lean against the counter for support.

Damn it, she wasn't going anywhere. This was her home, she'd built a place for herself here. She wouldn't be driven away by the crazy notion that a dead man had come back to life. Hank Rand was toasting in hell, not attending stock car races.

An almost overpowering need to call Keith washed over her and she grabbed the phone before she could stop herself. She had his number on Grace's application form. No doubt he was still on the road with Grace, but she could reach him on his cell phone.

If he could just hold her, wrap those powerful arms around her. Stroke her hair with those strong fingers, and murmur in her ear that she'd be fine, he was there to protect her.

Resolutely Sara folded up the piece of newspaper, tucked it back in her address book and headed toward her office. She had student reports to type up and a few bills to pay. The mundane tasks would keep her too distracted to worry.

It almost worked. She managed to keep the frightening memories at bay—those years with her father, the twelve short months with Victor in which kindness escalated to cruelty in imperceptible increments. When her mind threatened to wander in dangerous directions, she quickly brought it back in line with mental exercise.

But Keith proved a more stubborn train of thought. His face kept popping up, like a screen saver on her computer display. His blue eyes hot with passion or soft with kindness. His mouth parting as he prepared to kiss her or curved in a gentle smile.

But that was a complete fantasy. She couldn't remember ever seeing Keith smile. That realization only led to another—that she wanted nothing more than to put a smile on his sober face.

Stopping for dinner proved to be a waste of time; she barely ate a bite. A pang of loneliness lay heavy in her stomach, stealing her appetite. If Keith had been there with her, maybe she could have eaten something, maybe his presence would have soothed the ache inside her.

What if things had been different? What if she'd had a different kind of father, had never met Victor? If she'd somehow seen the monster behind those seemingly kind eyes and had walked the other way before he could so much as touch her?

Would she be able to trust Keith now? Could she let him kiss her, put his hands on her body, feel the desire build without fighting the fear that always seemed coupled with it?

What if he could heal her? What if by simply giving her body over to him, she could cleanse herself of the terror once and for all? That would be worth any price, to be a normal woman, to find joy in the touch of a man.

He'd come closest to giving her pleasure without fear. The few times they'd kissed, he'd been gentle, kind, had stopped the instant she'd asked.

So had Victor. But hadn't that felt different? Wasn't Victor more demanding, more insistent, even from the start? She couldn't seem to view the memory clearly.

When she laid down that night, she knew she wouldn't sleep. But she turned out the light anyway, stretched out in bed, the open window letting in dark, lonesome sounds—the wind sifting through the trees, the occasional soft whicker of a horse, the distant shrill of crickets.

And when she did sleep, uneasy dreams devolved into recurrent nightmares—her father chasing her, his heavy breathing growing louder, closer. His fingers brushing her shoulder, his voice rasping out, *I'll get you, girl!*

But near morning, the dream changed, a light up ahead showing her a door she'd never noticed before. Somehow she knew safety lay just beyond. Pushing her legs to move faster, she made for that sanctuary and passed through the threshold, running headlong into Keith's arms.

Chapter Ten

On Friday, Keith hustled like crazy to put the finishing touches on the barn before camp ended for the day. He'd squeezed in the construction of the wash rack over the two weeks he'd been here, putting in the concrete pad, setting the posts where the horses could be tied while they were hosed off on a hot summer day. The plumbing still had to be run out there from the water source by the arena and run to the barn as well. But he'd lined up a buddy with an irrigation business to do the work, gratis.

The coat of paint he was putting on the barn siding was the last job to complete. He'd finished the exterior this morning and had a good start on the interior. He'd worked through lunch, gulping down a sandwich and soda while he painted. It was barely one and it looked like he'd be done by three.

So once he walked out of here today, he was scot-free. He wouldn't have to come back to the ranch, see Sara every day, battle the almost unbearable impulse to touch her, to hold her. He would be out of sight, she'd be out of mind and he could forget all about her.

Fat chance of that. But at least he wouldn't be tempted spending his day so close to her, wrestling with the demons he'd thought he'd put to rest.

He'd become preoccupied with thoughts of his late wife, Melissa. Recalling the accident that killed her. The man in the car with her. And the reason they were together.

He would have sworn he'd laid to rest the turmoil of Melissa's death and the agony of the aftermath. But with Alicia Thorne back in his life, coupled with the intensity of his feelings for Sara, some days he didn't know which end was up. And somehow, the old questions were plaguing him again.

Had he and Melissa just been wrong for each other? He'd certainly messed up as a father—had he not been a good enough husband, either? He and Melissa had gone astray somewhere along the line, and not just with Christopher's death. Which was the first bad step?

It had been so long ago, it was hard to remember. They'd started dating twelve—no, thirteen years ago, although he'd known her longer than that.

She'd been three years behind him in high school, so he'd scarcely noticed her then. Then she'd gone to college back east, returning to open a C.P.A. practice in Marbleville. He'd been so damn busy getting his own business off the ground, he'd barely been aware that she'd returned to town.

Then one day he'd looked up from his breakfast at Nina's Café to see her smiling down the counter at him. It turned out she'd been eating at Nina's every morning in hopes of catching his eye.

She'd been sweet and pretty and soft-spoken, so feminine that opening doors for her and buying her flowers seemed as natural as breathing. She was biddable as well, going along with whatever he wanted, adamant about only one thing in their marriage.

Babies. She wanted at least three, maybe more if they could manage it. And she wanted them right away, wanted to start their family the first year of their marriage.

A scream of laughter snagged his attention and he glanced out the barn door to see Jeremy tearing past the tack room toward the arena. Sara went after him, calling his name, telling him to slow down. The horses, camped out in the cool shade of the arena, spooked, and trotted off a few steps. Keith watched Sara as she caught up to Jeremy and went down on one knee to talk to him.

Would Christopher have been as brimming with energy as Jeremy? He'd been an active child at age two, right up until the meningitis took him. He might have been running after the horses, too, too full of life to slow down.

Maybe if Christopher hadn't died, or Melissa's uterine infection after his birth hadn't made her sterile. Or maybe if Keith had only pulled himself out of his own grief enough to be a comfort to her. Or if they'd never met Rob and Alicia at the Lamaze class. Would it have changed anything?

To hell with what-ifs. They'd only make him crazy.

Setting the brush across the paint can, he strode down the barn aisle to where he'd left his bottle of water. As he lifted it to take a drink, the shuffle of feet turned him around. Sara stood just inside the barn door, hesitating there as if unsure of her welcome.

The trouble was, she was far too welcome. He wanted to close the distance between them, take her in his arms, kiss that mouth he burned to taste again. Never mind that he was speckled with paint and exhausted from working in the heat, that a sheen of sweat lay across her bare shoulders and along her collarbone. He would have gladly taken her right there in one of the stalls, if she was willing.

He finished taking his drink. "Did you need something?"

She moved closer, and in the dim coolness of the barn, he thought he saw something in her face, maybe an invitation. Then she blushed and turned away. "Did you speak to Alicia today?"

The question caught him off guard. "I've been working all day. When would I have talked to her?"

She didn't like his sharp tone; her lush mouth compressed with disapproval. "She left a message to say she'd wrangled a few hours off work. She'll be picking up Grace today."

That shouldn't hurt. Grace had been nothing more than a silent passenger beside him in the truck these past few weeks. But he'd miss the little girl's company nonetheless. "That'll give me a little more time to work."

She nodded. "When you're done, come down to the house. I want to give you a flyer for the picnic."

Damn. He'd forgotten entirely. Bad enough spending another day with Sara, dealing with the temptation to touch her, but Alicia would be there, providing yet another reminder of the ugliness of the past.

But that seemed like a damn cowardly reason not to attend. "Still not sure if I can go. I'll be finishing up today."

"You won't be back on Monday then?"

Was that regret in her eyes? "My business can't run itself."

But it hadn't had to with Wyatt working the three building sites. What the young man could handle on his own, he didn't bother Keith with. At the same time, he wasn't shy about asking for help when he needed it. In fact, Wyatt could probably oversee the finish work on those three sites, leaving Keith free to get underway on Delacroix's next project.

Head tipped down, she crossed her arms around her middle. "That's best."

Of course it was. So why did he have a knot in his gut? "How's it going with Grace?"

She shrugged. "I'd like to say she's been improving. She's smiling now. That's more than I could say when she first arrived. But she still won't speak. Still doesn't laugh." Sara fixed him with her gaze. "I don't know much more about what's ticking inside her than when she started here."

He heard her unspoken query. "There's nothing else I can tell you."

"Her father died in a car accident," Sara said. "She hasn't spoken since."

"That's all I know." It wasn't quite all, but what relevance could his wife's relationship with Grace's father have to her reluctance to speak? He damned well didn't want to bring up that nastiness for no reason. "So she won't be going another week?"

Sara shook her head. "No point." She turned back toward the door. "Don't forget the flyer before you leave."

He watched her head back down the hill, then picked up the paintbrush again. With his heartbreak reeling inside him like a hurricane, each stroke, up-down, up-down, helped hold the pain in check.

It was nearly five by the time he finished. Grace had come up the hill to the barn to give him a goodbye hug, clinging to him for a long time. Then he watched as she went with her mother over to Dudley's paddock and rubbed the old gelding's face over and over before she finally turned and trudged down the hill.

After putting away his painting supplies in the truck, Keith washed his hands at the spigot by the arena and gave one last look at the barn. The siding glowed a rich red in the late-afternoon sun, the color a near match for Sara's hair. He'd left the remaining half-can of paint by the tack room. She could use it for touch-ups and besides, he didn't need any reminders of her.

Swiping his hands dry on his jeans, he started toward the house. The prospect of stepping into her space, her home, seemed far too intimate.

He knocked, then bent to unlace his boots. She still hadn't answered by the time he'd slipped them off, so he knocked again, louder. Finally he heard the sound of footsteps approaching, the door latch releasing.

She'd been napping. Her unbound hair lay mussed around her face, hanging just past her shoulders. He'd never seen it down and its silkiness took his breath away. With her sleepy eyes and soft parted lips, she was some kind of erotic dream.

"Come on in," she said, stepping aside.

If she'd known how hard he was, the thoughts running rampant through his brain, she would have locked the door in his face. He was a grown-up for God's sake, and not some randy teenager. But he'd have to muster a hell of a lot of willpower to keep from reaching for her.

Barefoot, she padded into the kitchen. "Iced tea?"

"Sure, thanks." He stood behind the breakfast bar to hide the evidence his jeans couldn't conceal. "You said something about a flyer?"

She filled two glasses with ice and set them on the counter. "Right there."

He tugged the printed sheet toward him and made a show of reading it. He might as well at least pretend he might go. "So what would I bring?"

As she poured iced tea, he stared at the sheen of sweat across her chest. A vivid image popped into his mind—drawing his tongue along her collarbone, tasting every salty inch.

She slid the glass across the counter. "If you'll help Jameson barbecue hamburgers and hot dogs, you don't have to bring anything."

Lifting the iced tea, he took a long drink, half surprised

his body's heat didn't set it to boiling. The glass drained, he set it on the counter. "Maybe I'll see you tomorrow then." He put a hand on the flyer to pick it up.

She reached across the counter and grabbed his wrist. What he saw in her face—fear, hope, desire—didn't make sense. But her touch against his skin wiped out coherent thought anyway.

Keeping the contact, she stepped around the counter and just about into his arms. His heart pounded in his ears, a thunderous noise. When she released his wrist, she pressed her hands against his chest, running them up to his shoulders, curling around the back of his neck.

She tugged him down, tipping her face up, her lips parting. He ought to be noble and pull away, disengage those warm hands from around his neck. Leave before he did something they'd both regret. But then she brushed her body against his, her full breasts grazing his chest, and the chance for nobility was gone.

He slid his hands around her waist, pulling her tightly against him. She tensed, went completely rigid for a moment, and he thought he'd be putting the brakes on after all. But with a long breath, she relaxed, her muscles soft and pliable again.

The faint lavender scent of her, her heat under his hands clamored inside him, filling him with need. He wanted his mouth on every inch of her, to taste every curve, every dark corner. Pressing his lips against hers, the softest, barest kiss, he struggled to keep himself in check, to take things slow.

But she was tugging his T-shirt from his jeans, pushing

it up, urging him to strip it off. He obliged, but had his first inkling that something wasn't right here. There was a desperation in Sara's frantic actions, an edge out of sync with what should have been sensual.

The moment his T-shirt hit the floor, her fingers were at his belt, working at the buckle. In the process, her wrist skimmed against the placket of his jeans, knocking the breath clean out of him. He wanted to grab her hand, press it up against him, thrust against her palm.

He grabbed her wrists. "Wait."

Eyes wide, she stared up at him. He saw it again—the fear mingled with longing. What the hell was going on here?

Turning her hands, she took his and urged him toward the hall. "My bedroom," she said, barely a whisper.

He followed, too dazed with arousal to refuse. She backed down the short hall and into her bedroom door, leading him to her bed. She reached for the button of her denim shorts, couldn't seem to get her hands to work properly to unfasten it. Giving up, she yanked her tank top free and threw it aside. Sitting on the end of the bed, she scooted back toward the pillows, one hand beckoning.

If his mind was muddled before, now it froze, riveted on her gorgeous breasts. Her nipples were dark inside the plain white bra and his hands itched to stroke them. He tightened his hands into fists to hold back the urgency.

Her gaze dropped to his hands and now full-blown panic erupted in her face. She concealed it quickly enough, dragging her focus higher, forcing a smile. Despite the blood beating in his veins, he held back. "Sara—"

"Come here," she whispered. "Please."

He'd have to be insane to refuse. And yet…the uncertainty in her face was telling him something. Maybe just that it had been a long time for her, that she was out of practice.

But why was she doing this at all? How did they go from a few kisses to hot and heavy in bed? She'd done her best to keep him at arm's length, had never quite relaxed under his touch. What had changed?

"Please," she said again, barely audible.

Not at all sure of what he was doing, he lay beside her on the bed, leaving his jeans on. She immediately wrapped her arms around him, pressed her mouth against his, but there wasn't any passion in it. When he didn't kiss her back, she covered his fly with her hand and squeezed. The explosion of sensation nearly drove him clean out of his mind, but he gasped in a breath and pulled her hand away.

She tried to kiss him again, but he edged out of reach. He wouldn't let go of her hand to let her touch him, wouldn't let her get closer. He thought she might get mad, say something nasty to him.

She burst into tears.

At first he just lay there, stunned. Then he took her in his arms, tucking her head against his shoulder. As he stroked her thick, silky hair, her tears wet his skin and her body trembled.

The air conditioner cycled on and the cool air goosepimpled his flesh, despite the warm body next to his. Reaching past her, he tugged the bedspread loose and pulled it over them both. She quieted, sobs easing until she lay silent in his arms. Her breathing grew steadier, deeper, then to his surprise, he realized she was asleep.

His chest tightened, her sweetness overwhelming him. Despite the need that still burned inside him, he wanted nothing more than to hold her as long as she'd let him. Her presence eased him, soothed him. He hadn't felt so at peace since before the death of his only child.

The sun had dipped low enough that the tallest pines filtered its light, shading Sara's room. His arousal faded into languor, his limbs growing heavier, his eyes closing. Sara shifted, fitting herself more tightly against him, sighing with complete relaxation. A few minutes later, he drifted into sleep himself.

Something warm and firm lay beneath her cheek. In the dark of the room, in the first few moments of fuzzy awareness, she couldn't quite process why her pillow felt so comfortably different. Then, bit by bit, she came fully awake, and soon was mortified.

What had she done?

She lay there, motionless, listening to his deep, steady breathing. One of his arms cushioned her head, the other lay loosely over her waist. Her face was against his chest, her mouth close to his flat nipple.

She couldn't believe she'd followed through with such an idiot idea. Yes, he'd woken her from a sound sleep, had walked into her house looking incredibly male and utterly appealing. And yes, the ghost of her father still seemed to be chasing her, shaking up her life just as he had when she was a child.

Even so, she'd never intended to follow through with the aimless reverie of last night. Maybe in her fantasies, Keith's lovemaking would sweep away the ingrained barriers her body maintained, and she would suddenly be a complete woman. But reality had blown away that fairy tale. She'd shut down just as she always did.

And she'd cried in his arms. That seemed the greatest shame.

She tensed in anticipation of escaping from her embarrassment while Keith still slept. But his eyes snapped open and his hand on her back held her in place. Panic surged—she was trapped, he wouldn't release her—then his hand relaxed and he pulled it away.

His other arm still a warm pillow, he stared at her warily. "Are you okay?"

She couldn't face him. Pushing aside the covers, she slid from the bed and tried to remember where in the dark room her tank top might be. Her foot brushed against it on the floor by her desk. With her back to him, she put it on.

The bedside light went on and she squinted against the glare. She wrapped her arms around herself, feeling far too vulnerable.

"What's going on, Sara?"

She glanced over her shoulder at him. He was sitting up, leaning against one of her pillows. The contrast of his tanned skin against the pristine white of her pillowcase was mesmerizing. She could still remember the feel of his heat against her palms, the texture of his muscles as she ran her hands across his chest.

"Oh, Lord," she murmured. "I'm so sorry."

"Sit down," he said with a trace of irritation. "Talk to me."

She kept her bare feet firmly planted. "Can't we just pretend this never happened?"

"Sit," he said more sharply.

Cautiously she settled on the foot of the bed, bringing her legs up to sit cross-legged. She still couldn't look his way. "I never cried for him. Not once. Not for Victor, either."

He repositioned himself, crossing his legs as well, one knee nearly brushing against hers. "Make some sense, Sara."

Summoning courage, she lifted her gaze to his. "My father started hitting me a week after my mother died."

His sudden tension sent a skitter of fear through her. She could see his anger. "How old were you?"

"Nine. My sister Ashley was five."

"Did he hit her, too?"

"Just the one time." And they'd left that same night. "I made sure I was his only punching bag."

"Did he ever—"

"No. My father never touched me that way." Her stomach clenched. "But sometimes his friends…they would look at me…it was almost worse than being touched, wondering what they were thinking about me. And one of them…" She hadn't allowed herself to think about that hideous night in years, hadn't spoken of it to anyone.

"Tell me, Sara." His kindness unraveled the shame.

She gulped in air. "When I was thirteen, one of my father's cronies—" for a moment, she couldn't continue, had to force the rest out "—climbed into my bed."

He spoke so softly, she could barely hear. "Did he rape you?"

"His hands were everywhere. He tried to pull my pajamas off." It might as well have been yesterday, the images were so clear—the feel of that body, so heavy she couldn't breath, the stench of sweat and booze. "Before he could...he passed out. Too drunk."

He drew a finger across her cheek, an amazing comfort. "And Victor?"

She clenched her hands, hating the memories. "You would think the daughter of an abuser would know another abuser when she saw one."

Again that tension, that thread of anger. It wasn't directed at her, but she had to push down the knee-jerk fear nevertheless.

"What did he do?" He said the words softly.

"I thought he loved me." Ridiculous tears threatened, when she'd never before cried about Victor. "He seemed kind and caring..."

"But he hit you."

"I never saw it coming." She swiped the wetness from her cheeks. "He changed so slowly. Or maybe he took his time showing his true colors. Not at all like my father—dear old Dad could have been the poster boy for domestic batterers."

"How long were you with Victor?"

"A year." Self-disgust settled in her belly. "It only got bad at the end."

But that wasn't really true. When she looked back on those twelve months, she realized the strain between them started early on. She'd done everything she could to change herself as his behavior changed, becoming a little less outspoken, a little more demure in her dress, each day excusing more and more.

"When he hit me the first time, I thought…" Her throat tightened. "I can't believe I thought…that it was a mistake. That he didn't mean to."

"Don't blame yourself."

"Then the second time…can you believe it?" She laughed, a harsh, dark sound. "I nearly forgave him again. And I'd gone to the support groups, I'd taken the classes."

His first touch on her shoulder startled her, but then its gentleness soothed her. "It's not your fault."

"That's what they say." She couldn't seem to resist leaning toward him and his arm around her shoulders eased away some of the pain inside her. "I waited until he'd gone to work, then I grabbed as much of my stuff as I could and threw it in the car."

His fingers moved along her arm in comforting strokes. "He didn't come after you?"

"I'd struck up a friendship with a cop in one of my classes. He paid Victor a visit and made it clear what the consequences would be if he bothered me again."

"And your father?"

"Dead." She said it firmly to remind herself it was true. "His body was burned beyond recognition in a house fire."

They sat quietly, side by side, the air conditioner's hum the only sound. She ought to turn it off, open the window to let in the cooled night air. But Keith's warmth felt too good.

He caressed her shoulder. "Why did you kiss me?"

His question pushed her to her feet, drove her from the room. He followed, of course, his determined expression telling her he wouldn't let this go easily. And she just wished she could bury the entire incident a hundred feet underground.

She reached for the front door. "It's late. You should go."

He didn't move, just stood there like some kind of dazzling Greek statue. "Sara—"

"It was stupid," she blurted out. "Can't we just leave it at that?"

He took a step toward her, hand outstretched. Even knowing he didn't intend to hurt her, she recoiled. "Sorry," she said, near tears again.

"Damn it, don't apologize!"

"Then stop being angry." She swallowed back the tears. "When you're angry, I can't…"

Realization flashed in his eyes. He looked away, jaw set, then he bent to pick up his T-shirt. As he pulled it on, Sara sagged in relief. He would leave now; he would let it go.

But then he pulled a stool out from the breakfast bar and sat down. His intense gaze fixed on her for three long beats.

Sara hugged her middle. "It's late," she tried again.

"Tell me." His harsh voice gentled. "Please."

She realized he wasn't going anywhere until she did.

Taking in a deep breath, she struggled to frame the words. "With Victor, sex wasn't…good. Especially toward the end. I couldn't respond. It…hurt."

Emotions flickered in Keith's face—the anger, only for an instant, then a compassion that gave her courage. She forced herself to dredge up the ugly memories. "I always thought it was me. He made it clear he thought the same."

"Then he was a damn sick bastard." He said it mildly enough, but she saw the fire in his eyes. "You still believe that crap?"

"I haven't experienced anything since to convince me otherwise."

"You're telling me every man you've been with—"

"I haven't been with another man. Not since Victor. No one before him, either."

"But when you've kissed another man—"

"I can't let go. Can't feel what a woman should. But with you…I felt safe, so I thought…" A flush warmed her cheeks and she had to look away a moment. "I thought I'd try…to see if I could…"

"Respond."

"Yeah." She could barely squeeze it out.

"Without telling me."

"What difference would that have made?"

He pushed off the stool. "I'm not the one to fix you, Sara."

"I didn't expect you to."

"You need someone who cares about you. Who's willing to love you."

Love. The word thumped in her chest. To have a man

truly love her. She wished it were possible for someone like her.

"That isn't me." Now he looked angry again, but at himself. "Not me." He started for the door.

She grabbed the flyer from the counter. "Keith." She held it out to him. "Please."

For a moment he wouldn't take it. Then with obvious reluctance, he plucked it from her hand.

After he'd left, she sank onto the seat he'd vacated, wishing she could vanish from the face of the earth. If not for the children who counted on her, she was half tempted to pack up everything she owned and disappear down the road.

At least she'd confirmed something tonight. Despite her longing to the contrary, she was far too messed up to enjoy intimacy with a man. The debacle with Keith had made that very clear.

Chapter Eleven

Keith pulled into Marbleville County Park just as Mark Henley, owner of the Hart Valley Inn, and Jameson O'Connell were wrestling a massive barbecue grill from the back of Mark's pickup truck. Keith lent some muscle power to the task and the three of them rolled the awkward wheeled contraption down a ramp to the ground. As Mark took off, Keith helped Jameson guide the grill down the path to the picnic grounds.

Pulling from the front, Jameson glanced back at him. "So you've finished everything at the ranch?"

"Other than getting Scott over to run the water to the wash rack."

"Did Sara mention the addition to the house?"

He didn't like the direction the conversation was going. "I can't put in any more time over there."

"This wouldn't be a freebie. My grandmother would be providing the funding."

The path curved through a grove of oaks and led them to a clearing already seething with activity. The dozen or so kids from the camp sessions crisscrossed the picnic grounds, along with what looked like another couple dozen of their siblings. Their parents looked on or led the kids in games or set up food on the redwood picnic tables.

As if someone had installed radar in his brain, Keith immediately located Sara over by the water fountain. Her back to him, she was helping a toddler get a drink.

He and Jameson got the barbecue grill positioned near the tables. "Give me a hand with the charcoal?"

One last look at Sara, then he trudged back up the path with Jameson. If he thought his friend had given up on the notion of him doing more work at the ranch, he was disappointed.

"We've already got the drawings done," Jameson said. "The permits have been pulled. The money's in place."

"I've got another job coming down the pike."

"You have the permits?"

Jameson knew too damn much about the construction business. "Not yet." And the way the county was running behind, it would be another four weeks.

Back in the parking lot, they grabbed the four twenty-pound bags of charcoal from Jameson's small truck, two bags each. "What do you think?" Jameson prodded.

"I'll think about it." Except all the thinking in the world wouldn't convince him to say yes. Especially after what had happened last night.

He would have given anything to take Sara back into that bedroom and show her the way her body could feel. But it was pure ego thinking he could get past the fear, the pain that bastard had inflicted on her. Yes, he knew how to go slow, be gentle, but after what Sara had been through it was extremely arrogant to think he was such a spectacular lover he could instantly solve her problems.

Even if he could, it would have been a monumental mistake. Women didn't respond to sex the way men did; somehow it always seemed to mean more to them than it did to guys. She might have started to think there was more between them than there really was, that something more was possible.

That he might love her.

A bead of sweat rolled between his eyes and he shook his head to throw it off, wishing he could throw off his thoughts of Sara as easily. Then he took that last turn of the path and there she was, at the picnic table next to the grill.

As he let the bags slide to the ground, she turned his way, her hair as usual escaping her ponytail, her shoulders bared by her grass-green tank top. Her khaki shorts ended just above her knees, but they might as well be cutoffs considering how his body responded to her dimpled knees and shapely calves. She wore sandals instead of the boots she protected her feet with around the ranch. Seeing her naked toes reminded him of last night, her standing barefoot in her living room just before she kissed him.

Her wary gaze fixed on him as he swiped his brow with the heel of his hand. Tearing open a package of napkins, she pulled a few out and offered them to him.

"Thanks," he told her as he dried his face. Probably a lost cause; he'd break out in a sweat again having her so near.

"Thanks for coming," she said softly. "I wasn't sure if you'd still want to."

What he wanted and what was wise weren't always the same thing, as he'd discovered this morning when he found himself in his truck on his way over before he'd really thought it through. He might tell himself it was for Grace's sake—that was at least part of the truth—but the long night of tossing and turning, obsessing over Sara was the real heart of the matter.

But he might as well pretend otherwise. "Grace here yet?"

"Alicia called. She's running late. Something about her boss being in a state of panic over some misplaced files."

He'd had only the briefest opportunity to touch her hair, to feel its silkiness against his palm. Now with the rich auburn curling around her face, he longed to run his hands over it, smooth it back, feel it slide against his skin.

He turned away abruptly. "I'll start loading up the coals."

Jameson had left his load beside the grill and had been waylaid by one of the dads who needed help bringing over coolers of sodas and hot dogs. Keith levered the grills off the half barrel shaped barbecue and leaned them against a nearby oak. Emptying the four bags, he rolled up the stiff paper and looked around for a trash.

Her fingers brushed his arm. "Over here," she said, indicating the metal trash can chained to a wooden post set in the ground.

He gathered up the bags and she opened the lid for him, still standing too close for comfort. Needles of anticipation prickled all over him, as if every cell in his body was tuned and ready for her next move.

"The coals need to be lit an hour or so before I start cooking."

She checked her watch and he wanted to press a kiss to the tender skin on her wrist. "Give it another half hour, then."

They just stood there, inches apart, everything inside him clamoring to reach for her, to touch her. He shoved his hands in the pockets of his denim shorts.

She sighed, the sound enticing. "Keith…" Glancing around her, she urged him away from the main ruckus. "Can we get past last night? I'm still about as mortified as I can be, but I'll get over it if we can just be…normal."

"I'm not sure we've ever been normal." He gave in to temptation and drew a strand of her hair behind her ear.

"I wish I knew how."

Her hand closed over his, started to pull it away. But then she brushed her mouth across his fingers, her hazel eyes softening before she let go.

She shook her head, her expression rueful. "I don't know what I'm doing."

He tipped her chin up. "Despite the fear, you can't deny the desire is there."

"No, I can't." She folded her arms around herself. "It's just useless."

A scream of laughter from the picnic grounds filtered through the trees. "I'd better get back." Sara moved around him and back toward the others.

He caught her hand, stopping her, turning her around. "Nothing you did last night should embarrass you. You're a sexy, desirable woman. Things happened to you that weren't your fault."

She gazed up at him. "We're okay, then?"

"Very okay."

Heat shot through him when she smiled. He could barely let go of her hand when she pulled away.

As he watched her through the trees, calling out to the children, gathering them for a game, he tried to sort out the firestorm inside him. His body wanted her desperately, that much was clear. But deeper inside him resided another kind of need, a tight little knot that wasn't quite pain, wasn't quite joy. If he let go of it, it might go one direction or the other, but if he was wrong and it went badly, the hurt would be excruciating.

He'd had enough experience with that kind of disaster. He'd invested love in his feckless mother and she'd left him. He'd trusted that life was fair and his son died. He'd believed that people were basically good and then discovered his wife's ultimate betrayal.

He checked his own watch and saw he still had fifteen minutes before he lit the coals. A path meandered through the trees and if he remembered correctly there was a creek at the end of it. He could use a few minutes beside the water, listening to its chatter over the rocks.

The significance of the date blinking on the face of his digital watch sank in. One year ago today. The accident. The call from Deputy Gabe Walker telling him his wife was dead. How the hell could he have forgotten?

He glimpsed Sara through the trees, her hair beautiful in the sunlight. The sight of her just sharpened the pain within him.

He started down the trail, holding on tight inside.

It was nearly lunchtime by the time Alicia showed up with Grace. The little girl immediately sought out Keith, but when she ran toward the smoking barbecue to give him a hug, he called out sharply, "Stop!" to warn her off. He immediately put down the spatula he'd been using to flip burgers and stepped clear of the hot grill, but the reprimand, however well-meaning, had thrown Grace back into herself. She stood stiffly as Keith hugged her, promptly breaking away.

Keith glanced over at Sara as he returned to his station behind the grill. "She could have burned herself."

"You did the right thing. She's just so fragile."

Alicia looked almost as lost, the slender blonde standing there with a pan of store-bought brownies in her hands. Sara smiled and gestured over to the picnic table where they'd been laying out the side dishes and desserts the parents had brought.

Sara met her at the far end of the table. "This is great. Only one other parent brought brownies." She reorganized the various pans and plates to make room for Alicia's contribution.

"They aren't homemade. I didn't have time." Alicia squeezed the foil pan between the lemon cake and platter of chocolate chip cookies.

"I'm just glad you're here."

Alicia scanned the grassy picnic area, no doubt searching out her daughter. She sighed with relief when she found Grace over by the swings, waiting her turn. "I almost didn't make it."

"Because of your boss?"

"Because of the date." Alicia pressed her lips together. "It's been a year."

"Since…" Understanding dawned. "Since her father died."

"We got the call right after dinner."

Over at the swings, Grace clung to one of the support posts, watching Jeremy arc back and forth. "I wanted to ask Jameson for another week," Sara said, keeping her gaze on Grace. "But she's made so little progress, it would be hard to justify. If I had some new angle, a new insight…"

Alicia stared at her daughter. "I just want her to talk to me again."

"Then tell me what you can. Even if it doesn't seem important." Sara held her breath. When she'd first interviewed Alicia, and with each progress report, she'd asked the woman essentially the same question. Each time Alicia had insisted she'd told her everything.

Beyond the delicate blonde, Keith watched them both from his station by the grill. A few children and adults had started lining up for their hamburgers and hot dogs. Before long, they'd be crowded around the picnic table, intruding on this moment with Alicia.

Taking the woman's hand, Sara walked along the perimeter of the picnic grounds with her. "Alicia…" she prompted.

Tears sheened Alicia's eyes. "It started that afternoon. Something she told me."

"What was it?"

She didn't want to answer. "The day care had gone into Marbleville for ice cream. Grace saw my husband..." She glanced across the picnic grounds toward Keith. "With a woman."

"They were..."

"Yeah." Alicia let out a heavy gust of air. "She saw them kissing. She knew it wasn't right, so she told me when I picked her up at the day care."

They'd reached the swings. All the other children clustered around the picnic tables, but Grace had hung back, taking her turn on the swing. She looked so alone, so cut off from everything around her, it set off an ache in Sara's heart.

"When my husband got home, we fought," Alicia continued. "It was loud and it was ugly. Turns out the affair had been going on for years." She shook her head. "I was such an idiot."

"Grace heard the fight?"

"She hid in her room, but she couldn't help but hear."

"Had she ever heard you fight before?"

Alicia shrugged. "A few times. Things weren't perfect between us." Another glance over at Keith.

He was busy serving hot dogs to the horde of kids, one after the other. As he turned to put more burgers on the grill, his gaze fixed on Sara. Was he concerned about what Alicia might be telling her?

Sara had to ask. "What about Keith?"

Alicia wouldn't look at her. "What about him?"

Did you two have a relationship? Sara burned to know, but if they had, she doubted it had anything to do with Grace's silence. "He's the only person besides you that your daughter shows any affection for."

Alicia's brow furrowed. "I honestly don't know why that is. She always liked him, even before…the accident. But then she hadn't seen him for nearly a year."

"What happened after the fight?"

Alicia drew in a shaky breath. "He went out. We never saw him again. That's really all I can tell you."

Frustration bubbled up inside Sara. They'd nearly come around again to the picnic tables and Sara felt as if the conversation had been just as circular. Grace had seen her father kiss another woman, had heard her parents fight, then her father had left the house and been killed in an accident. There was a piece missing, heck, there were probably several. But it didn't look as if she'd be shaking them out of Alicia.

They arrived at the grill just as Keith was serving himself a burger on a paper plate. He handed it to Alicia. "You take this one. There's a couple more almost ready." Grabbing a hot dog bun, he dropped a hot dog into it. "For Grace."

After piling on potato salad and coleslaw, Alicia took the plate over to the swings, no doubt to coax Grace to eat. Sara stood beside the grill with Keith as the burgers sizzled. "Where's Jameson?" she asked.

"Crisis at the café. A busload of tourists." He waved the spatula toward the picnic table. "If you could get a couple plates and buns, I'll serve these up."

She held them out as he slipped the patties on the bread. Then they shifted to the picnic table where the bounty had been reduced to dribs and drabs of food. They nabbed a couple cans of soda from the ice-filled cooler then carried their food and drink to an empty table.

He picked up his burger, but didn't eat it. "You and Alicia were talking."

She took a bite of potato salad, not sure how direct she should be. But she'd tired of dancing around the subject of Grace. "Did you know her husband was having an affair?"

She might as well have slammed him in the head with a rock. He stared at her, then glanced over at Alicia, eating with Grace near the swings.

"Yes." He hissed the word. "I damn well knew."

"You never told her?"

He slapped down the burger. "She told me. After the accident." He looked ready to chew nails. "Did she tell you with who?"

"I didn't ask. I didn't think it was pertinent."

"Pertinent." He spit the word out. "You mean it didn't add anything to your treasure trove of town gossip?"

She stared at him, caught between shock and anger. Anger won out and she felt ready to give him a shove. "I don't give a rat's behind about town gossip. You might have forgotten, but this is about Grace. Not you, not Alicia—Grace. Any information I gather is to help her."

He stood up, stomped a few paces away. Despite his obvious ire, Sara was surprised at her response—more irritation than fear. As impossible as it had seemed to come to trust Keith, somehow it had begun to happen, millimeter by millimeter.

When he turned back around, he'd composed himself, his anger dissipated. "You're right." He settled beside her again. "It's just that this is…personal to me."

"Because Alicia's a friend?"

"Because I care for Grace. Because…" She could see him struggle to speak. "Because of my own son."

Stunned, Sara tried to frame something sensible to say. "You have a son?"

"Had." His jaw worked, tension beating there. "Born around the same time as Grace. He died at age two."

"His mother—"

"Dead." He took a massive bite of his burger, no doubt hoping to cut off any more questions.

Her curiosity prodded her to ask, but she couldn't see what a child dead six years would have to do with Grace. So she focused on finishing her lunch, fetching the last two brownies for her and Keith. Then the kids, ramped up from cookies and cake, needed a diversion. Dividing them up into teams, they played Red Rover and Steal the Bacon.

Alicia and a few of the other parents cleaned up from lunch, tossing out the last bits of leftover food, consolidating what was left of the treats on a single plate. After he'd cooled the coals with buckets of cold water, Keith and Mark Henley took the grill back to Mark's truck. The exhausted children flocked around the picnic table one last time to devour the last of the cookies and cake.

As the parents gathered up their charges, they each stopped to thank Sara for her work with their children, remarked on the progress they'd made, and how much they'd enjoyed the picnic. Then the families headed out, the children chattering with excitement, until the crowd had thinned to her, Keith and Alicia.

Tossing the last paper plate, Alicia brushed off her hands and smiled at Sara. "I'd better get Grace home."

Sara took a look around. "Is she in the car?"

"By the swings—" Alicia stopped short. "Maybe she headed toward the parking lot with everyone else." She trotted off, then shouted back over her shoulder. "Will you stay here? In case she comes back this way?"

"We'll take a quick look around," Sara said, starting toward the swings. Two trails led off into the trees beyond.

"You take that path to the right," Keith suggested. "I'll take the one to the left."

They both took off at a run, shouting Grace's name. There was no sign of the little girl along the right-most path, which narrowed to a deer trail as it meandered through the woods.

As she considered whether to continue on through the brush, she heard Keith's shout. "Sara!"

Thinking he'd found her, she backtracked, then hurried along the path Keith had taken. She found him standing beside a fallen log. There was a half-eaten brownie already swarming with ants.

"I found this, too," Keith said, holding out a square of paper. It was a photograph of a man, smiling at the camera.

"Who is it?" Sara asked, although she registered the familiarity of the man's features.

"Rob Thorne," Keith said. "Grace's father."

* * *

Alicia returned from checking the car in a near panic and when Keith showed her the photo, it pushed her completely over the edge. Sara took her hand, even though she knew Alicia would find scant comfort in the gesture. Despite Keith's assurance that Grace probably hadn't gone far, Alicia was on the edge of tears.

Sara squeezed her hand. "When did you see her last?"

"I thought it was her by the swings," she gasped out, "as everyone was gathering up to leave. But that might have been Jeremy's sister. She's got the same color hair."

Keith asked, "Then you're not sure how long she's been gone?"

"No." Alicia sobbed, then swallowed it back. "God, I can't even recognize my own child."

Keith started toward the parking lot. "Cell phone's in the truck. I'd better call Gabe." The deputy sheriff would contact the Marbleville County Search and Rescue.

Sara rubbed Alicia's back. "We were all busy, the kids were running around everywhere. It was an honest mistake."

"What does that matter if she's lost?"

Keith returned shortly, cell phone in hand. "Gabe and Tom Jarret are hauling over four horses." He turned to Sara. "I'm assuming you'll ride with us."

"I have a pair of jeans and boots in my car. I'll change while we're waiting."

In the thirty minutes it took Gabe and Tom to arrive, Keith extended his previous search, calling out for Grace before returning to continue the search on horseback. By then, Alicia was nearly hysterical. Fortunately Tom had had the foresight to bring his wife Andrea with them. Andrea had taught Grace last year at Hart Valley Elementary and understood the little girl as well as anyone. Alicia immediately went into Andrea's comforting embrace.

With Andrea's assistance, Gabe questioned Alicia about when and where she'd last seen Grace while Tom, Keith and Sara quickly tacked up the horses. Another group was on its way to fan out and search on foot; Andrea would organize them when they arrived.

As they rode toward the picnic grounds, Gabe led the way. "Alicia's certain she saw Grace after lunch. She left her by the swings when she went to throw away their trash."

"That would be one or one-thirty then," Sara said, then checked her watch. "It's nearly four. How far could she have gone in three hours?"

Riding in twos, they started down the trail where they'd found the photograph. Not far past the fallen log, the path split and she and Keith took the left branch while Tom and Gabe took the other.

"She's probably fine," Keith said, but Sara could hear the worry in his tone.

"Where does this path lead?" Sara asked.

"Down to the canyon eventually. It gets pretty rocky and steep."

So Grace could easily take a wrong step and end up tumbling to the bottom. Sara couldn't think about that; she had to focus on her surroundings, search for any sign of the little girl. She kept her gaze moving through the trees, along the ground.

"My son was pretty good at wandering off." Keith cleared his throat. "The moment he learned to walk."

It seemed such a miracle that Keith was willing to talk about his son, she wanted to keep the conversation going. "Where did he go?"

"Out the back door and off into the fields behind the house. Melissa would forget to lock the door and off he'd go. I'd hear the back door slam and go out on the back porch to keep an eye on him." The trail narrowed briefly and he reined his horse in to let her past, then caught up. "Bugs fascinated him. And rocks. He was always bringing home a pocketful."

Sara could imagine a small carbon copy of Keith, with those brilliant blue eyes. "He sounds like a great kid."

"Drove Melissa crazy. She didn't like him leaving like that." ·

"She wanted him safe."

"She was afraid of black widows and rattlers." He laughed, a hollow sound. "In the end, we couldn't keep him safe."

Sara hadn't even known the child, but her throat tightened with tears. "I'm so sorry, Keith."

"It'll be six years next month. All that time, you'd think I'd stop missing him so much."

"How could you?" Sara asked. "He was your son."

His hand gripped the saddle horn, looked ready to tear the leather right off. The gelding under him sensed the tension in Keith's body and skittered a few steps. Keith pulled him back alongside Sara.

Halting the horse, he dropped the knotted reins over the saddle horn. "Why the hell am I talking about this?"

"Sometimes it's better to talk."

"It only hurts. And I'm damn tired of the pain."

Sara edged her mare closer, dropping her own reins. Grief weighted Keith's shoulders, scarred his face with sorrow. When she put her hand over his, still tight around the saddle horn, he turned to her, his expression so fierce it frightened her. But then his hand relaxed, capturing hers gently for a moment before urging his horse forward, only glancing back to make sure she was behind him.

A massive boulder up ahead squeezed the path into single file again, the trail descending sharply in a switch-back beyond it. As they came even with the boulder, Keith's gaze fixed on something at the base of the immense rock.

He slid from the horse and handed the reins over to Sara, then climbed back up the hill. Pushing aside the brush, he dug something out from a large crevasse in the granite.

"What is it?" Sara asked.

He held up a small pink sneaker. "Is it hers?"

"I think she was wearing pink today."

He examined the dust of the trail. "There's a long skid here. She must have slipped, then had to pull her foot out of her shoe to get free."

"She can't have gone too much farther with only one sneaker."

Keith mounted his horse again and they continued down the rocky trail that grew steeper with each switch-back. Sara's horse stumbled several times and Keith's nearly went to its knees on the difficult path.

Keith climbed from the saddle. "We'd better leave the horses here."

Looping the reins over a low branch, they resumed their perilous descent. Sara's feet nearly went out from under her when the rocks she trod on shifted. Keith's hand steadied her until she could get her balance. Sara peered through the trees. "Could she have gotten this far without…" *Without falling. Please don't let her have fallen.*

He cupped his hands around his mouth. "Grace!"

They listened to the silence. "Would she even answer?"

"You call her," Keith said.

Sara drew in a breath. "Grace!" No answer. "Grace, are you here?"

Not a sound but the breeze teasing the leaves on the trees. Then, so softly, Sara thought it might have been a breeze… "Sara?"

She and Keith exchanged a quick glance. "Grace! Call out again!"

"Sara!" This time, the little girl screamed the name.

"Over there," Keith shouted, and he cut across the switchback trail to a clump of manzanita below. Sliding and skidding in the oak leaves and pine needles, he reached the red-branched shrub just as Grace stepped clear.

The little girl nearly jumped into his arms, clinging to his neck as he picked her up. "I'm sorry," she sobbed as if her heart were breaking, "I'm sorry."

Chapter Twelve

Once they got back to the horses, Grace surprised Sara by insisting on riding with her instead of Keith. Sitting behind the saddle on the mare's rump, the little girl wrapped her arms so tightly around Sara's waist, Grace just about squeezed the breath out of her.

Sara sent a silent signal Keith's way, indicating he should ride up ahead a bit. If Grace had anything else to say, Sara wanted to make sure she had the privacy to say it to Sara alone.

"What were you sorry about, Grace?" Sara prodded. "That you got lost?"

Her warm face was pressed tight to Sara's back. Grace spoke so softly, she was barely audible. "No."

"Can you tell me?"

Grace leaned around Sara, looking up ahead at Keith. Then she settled against Sara's back again. "It's my fault."

"What is, sweetheart?"

She took a ragged breath. "That Daddy died."

No assurance that it wasn't her fault would help Grace now. Better to just let her talk it out. "What do you mean?"

"I told Mommy about Daddy kissing Aunt Melissa. They had a big fight and he drove away." Her voice lowered to a whisper. "I shouldn't have told Mommy."

Something Grace had said had led to her father's death, so the little girl had decided it was better not to speak. In the eight-year-old's mind, it made perfect sense.

"You thought your Mom should know about your Dad and your aunt."

"She wasn't really my aunt, I just called her that. Like Uncle Keith isn't really my uncle."

There was something in the seemingly unrelated information that sent Sara's antenna up. *Drove Melissa crazy. She didn't like him leaving like that.* Rob Thorne was having an affair with Keith's wife?

Sara sat there, stunned, staring at Keith's back as his horse climbed the hill ahead of her. The pieces fell into place—the connection he had with Alicia that he wouldn't discuss, the odd closeness of his relationship with Grace. If she called him "Uncle Keith," she'd known him a long time, likely all her young life.

"You didn't make your daddy drive away, sweetheart," Sara told her. "You didn't make the accident happen."

"I shouldn't have tattled," Grace whispered. "I should have pretended I didn't see."

"You couldn't have saved your daddy no matter what you did, Grace. I'm so sorry he died."

"Me, too," she gasped out, then the sobs poured out of her. Her tears wet the back of Sara's tank top, the little girl's grief seemingly endless.

After a long time, she quieted, her body relaxing against Sara's. She jogged her horse up to Keith's, and they took the last of the trail side by side.

Shadows in his eyes, Keith asked Grace, "How are you doing, sweetheart?"

"I'm fine, Uncle Keith," Grace said solemnly.

His gaze locked with Sara's briefly, and she could see the questions there. But then they reached the fallen log where Gabe waited for them. By the time they reached the picnic area, more than a dozen people crowded around, everyone smiling, joyful that Grace had been found.

Grace slid from the horse into her mother's arms. Alicia sobbed with relief, clutching her daughter close. Then when Grace gasped out, "I love you, Mommy," Alicia sank to her knees in tears.

Back in the parking lot, Gabe gave Grace a quick once-over, then suggested Alicia take her over to Marbleville County Hospital to check her ankle. Sara took Alicia aside long enough to relay what Grace had told her, what had been the key to unlocking the little girl's voice. Then the buzz of conversation dwindled as people climbed into cars and Tom Jarret drove away his four-horse trailer.

Hands shoved in his pockets, Keith leaned against his truck parked down the row from Sara's car. Head down, he looked like he'd been sucker punched, so closed in on himself, it broke Sara's heart. There was no way she could just climb into her car and leave him.

He raised his head as she approached, turmoil hardening his features. Sara wasn't sure what was brewing inside him, had no idea what to say that might comfort him. So she didn't speak, just slipped her hands around his waist and put her arms around him. His body rigid, he didn't move, other than the rise and fall of his chest as he breathed.

"I can't let go," he whispered harshly. "It'll all blow up if I do."

She stroked the steel of his back, the tension unyielding under her hands. "If you want to talk to me—"

"What did she tell you?"

It might have been an unconventional counseling session with Grace, but it deserved confidentiality nonetheless. "I can't really say."

"She told you about Melissa." He said it matter-of-factly. "And her father."

She could tell him that much. "Yes."

He released a long, heavy sigh. Then, tentatively, as if he wasn't sure he should, he wrapped his arms around her and rested his chin on her head. His breath feathered her hair, warming her.

"Would you come home with me?" he asked. "I have something I want to show you."

"Yes." In that moment, she would do anything to soothe the agony inside him.

She followed in her car, the early-evening sun glaring in her rearview mirror. As she pulled into his driveway, the house and the fields beyond still simmering with the day's heat, it seemed the world held its breath in anticipation of what might come next.

With the curtains drawn and the air-conditioning running, his house was cool and dim, a relief after hours outside. Between her exertions during the picnic and the long ride searching for Grace, she felt sticky and grimy.

He motioned toward the living room with its plump cushioned sofas. "Have a seat."

"I'd probably leave a trail of dirt."

"You can shower if you like." There wasn't a shred of innuendo in his tone.

Even still, heat settled low in her body. "I can change back into my shorts and sandals, but I don't have another top."

"I didn't save anything of Melissa's." Shadows gathered in his eyes again.

"I don't have to shower."

"I'll give you one of my T-shirts. It's the first bathroom on the left. Go get your things and I'll leave the shirt in there for you."

He headed down the hall, still so wound up, she thought he might shatter if she touched him. She quickly retrieved the shorts and sandals she'd worn at the picnic, then returned to the house.

A skylight in the bathroom fed the sun's illumination into the room, so she left the light off. A neatly folded white T-shirt lay on the sink counter, Delacroix Construction imprinted on the front in red.

The shower felt heavenly, the warm spray washing

away the dust and smell of horse. She'd found a small sample bottle of shampoo under the sink and used half of it to lather her unruly hair. It took forever to get all the shampoo out, but it was worth it to feel clean.

The water pressure changed slightly and she realized Keith must be showering, too. Images poured over her—the water pounding his chest, rivulets coursing between his legs, wetting that mystery that she'd always feared before. But now, she could imagine with crystal clarity running her hand along its naked length, reveling in its hardness, its exquisite sensitivity.

Her nipples peaked, aching with sensation. For the first time in a long time, she wanted to touch herself, to experience her sexuality. Even more, she longed to have Keith touch her.

Shutting her mind to the fantasies as she shut off the water, she grabbed the plush towel waiting for her and stepped from the shower. She dabbed herself dry, still so self-aware she thought she'd burst from her own skin. It didn't help that she could hear the shower running elsewhere in the house, could still picture Keith naked under that spray.

She was loath to put her bra back on, but her breasts were too large to go braless under a T-shirt, no matter how loose. Her nipples brushing against the knit of Keith's T-shirt would be more than she could bear.

Dressed, but with the towel still wrapped around her hair, she padded barefoot back into the living room where she'd left her tote bag. Digging out the hairbrush, she unwound the towel, then started back toward the bathroom.

Keith emerged from a door across the hall from the bathroom, his hair damp, wearing nothing but jeans slung low on his hips. She'd barely had time to see his chest during their aborted folly last night. Now she looked her fill at the striated muscles of his shoulders, the taut lines of his belly bisected with dark hair curling to the waistband of his jeans.

He carried what looked like a book in his hands. His gaze fixed on her face a moment, then trailed down her body, the kind of examination that with another man, might have insulted her. But Keith only stoked her fire hotter, until she could barely breathe.

"I have to brush my hair," she told him, edging toward the bathroom.

"Let me," he said, setting the book down in the hall. He took the brush and towel from her, dropping the towel over the rack.

He positioned her in front of the mirror, standing behind her in the dimming light. She wanted to lean back against him, feel the warmth of his bare skin through the knit of the T-shirt she wore. But she stood motionless as he skimmed his hands over her wet hair.

The thick mass tumbled around her face, curls twisting in her eyes. He started in the back, carefully brushing from the bottom up toward the roots, easing out each snarl.

"I did this for Melissa before we were married, for a few years after." With a long stroke, he finished the back and gathered up another length of hair. "When she was pregnant with Christopher, it helped relax her."

It had the opposite effect on Sara. With each pass of the

brush through her hair, his fingers brushed her cheek or grazed her ear or drifted along her throat. She had to grip the edge of the sink to keep herself from pressing up against him.

"After Christopher…after he was gone, she barely let me touch her anymore."

She caught his empty hand and pressed a kiss into his palm. His eyes squeezed shut and his chin dropped to rest on her head. Then he tugged free and resumed his magic with the brush.

"When did she and Rob Thorne…"

His hands stilled for a moment, then his gaze lifted to hers in the mirror. "It started two or three months after Christopher died."

"Then they were together—"

"Five years, more or less." He laughed harshly. "Pretty clueless, wasn't I?"

"You were grieving."

"It should have brought us together."

"It doesn't always work that way."

"I couldn't let myself think. Couldn't let Christopher inside my brain." Raw pain edged his admission. "I worked. Ten-hour, twelve-hour days. I'd come home, fall into bed."

His hand faltered as he drew the brush smoothly through her thick auburn curls. "I worked. Melissa found her comfort with Rob."

Sara's heart ached in sympathy for those two anguished souls. There was nothing she could do for Melissa. But Keith was here, still just as lost in grief.

"I was so damn stupid," he said bitterly. "We made love so infrequently and when we did…she was never really there with me."

He took the last bit of tangled hair, focused on it as he spoke. "What I don't know…what Alicia doesn't know…is why they were together that night. If they were planning to go away together…if they were planning to break it off."

He'd finished brushing out the knots and now he ran his fingers through the wet strands, from scalp to tips. Each time his fingers dove in, they grazed her scalp, the sensation incredible. Sara's heart pounded in her ears.

She swallowed, her throat dry. "Would it have made a difference?"

His hands resting on her shoulders, he laid his cheek against her wet hair. "It doesn't matter now."

She turned, breaking his light hold on her. "Forgiving her would matter. Letting go of her betrayal."

Behind him, sunlight tinged with orange still poured into the small room, casting shadows on his face. "She's dead and gone. She means nothing to me anymore."

"Then why do you still hurt?" Sara whispered.

His gaze burned into her. The lines of his face seemed to sharpen in the half-light, as if the pain was rising to the surface, forcing its way out. He took a breath and she thought he might speak.

Instead he brought his hands up to cradle her face and lowered his mouth to hers. She couldn't help the spurt of fear, although with his first gentle touch, it eased away. His tongue tracing along her lower lip dispersed the last of it.

His thumbs brushed her ears, the bare contact sizzling along her spine. Then his hand took a leisurely path along her throat, her shoulder, the outside curve of her breast. The heat stole her breath, took the strength from her knees. In tandem with the pleasure his fingers gave, his kisses trailed from the corner of her mouth, along her jaw, to her ear, leaving sensation in their wake.

"I want you in my bed," he said hoarsely.

"Yes." Caution told her to think, to consider what she was doing. But the time for caution was over. "Yes," she said again.

He urged her from the bathroom, down the hallway, kissing her all the while. She focused on the warmth, the feel of him—the softness of his mouth, the firmness of his hands, his chest. She didn't want to let in the old, ugly memories, to have the deliciousness of the moment stop cold.

But when they got to his bedroom and he shouldered the door open, the panic tugged at her. She tried to ignore it, to push it down, but its grip was too strong. Her body stiffened, her fingertips pushing into his chest, her back rigid.

He felt it—how could he not? Pulling back from her, his face clearer in the flood of light from a myriad of windows, she saw the question in his eyes before he asked it. "Do we stop?"

The easy way would be to say yes. To walk away from his touch, his room, his house. To walk away from his life as well. She wouldn't have to see him after today, could pretend this interlude never happened.

But she couldn't leave. She couldn't turn her back on the possibility here. It wasn't love, it wasn't forever after. But if she could experience the kind of fulfillment that had always seemed a fantasy for her, she was willing to grab the opportunity.

"I want this," she said finally. "I want you."

He kissed her, his mouth lingering on hers, his tongue sweeping inside. "We go as slowly as you want. We stop if you want."

"I won't want to stop."

"You might."

"Then we pause." She found she could smile. "Take a break."

His gaze bored into her, the desire plain on his face. She stood close enough that she could feel his erection brushing against her thighs. Yet he would let her go if she asked.

He took her hands, drawing her into the room. It was plain and masculine, with a well-used heavy oak dresser and a woven rug on the hardwood floor. A navy comforter covered the bed, a mass of matching pillows spread across the carved wooden headboard. Windows filled the back wall and she could see the sky just beginning to darken at the far edge of his fields.

He guided her toward the head of the bed. Piling the pillows together, he sat against them and pulled her toward him, settling her in his lap. His arms circled her loosely, giving her a sense of freedom that kept the panic at bay.

She brushed a kiss across his lips. "Let me touch you."

He drew a finger along her face. "Please."

She indulged herself, exploring his body with her fingertips—the broad shoulders, the muscular chest, the powerful arms. She kept her forays above the waist, fascinated by the hard ridge under her hip, but still reluctant to take that next step. Instead she turned her attentions to his face, his freshly shaved cheeks, the firm line of his jaw, his parted lips.

As her fingers brushed across his mouth, he captured her hand, pressing a kiss into her palm, then drawing each fingertip inside. She shivered from the pressure of his mouth, his teeth gently grazing her fingers.

He took a handful of the T-shirt, pulling it from the waist of her shorts. "Okay?" he asked, hesitating.

The fear, however faint, still warred with sensation, but she refused to let it win. "Okay."

She wanted to wrench off the T-shirt, to plunge ahead. But she'd tried that last night and it had been a disaster.

Instead she focused on the feel of his fingertips stroking as he freed the hem of the T-shirt from her shorts, then pulled it up along her rib cage, touching her along the way. He lingered briefly to trail his thumbs along the sides of her breasts, this time circling nearer her nipples, hard nubs inside the cups of her bra.

He pulled the T-shirt over her head and her still-damp hair fell across her shoulders and down her back. The sudden chill against the bare skin of her back sent a shiver through her.

"Cold?" he asked as he ran fingers through her hair. The knuckles of his other hand stroked the underside of her breast, the motion mesmerizing.

She shook her head, too caught up in his touch to form

words. Even as she told herself they had to go slow, she burned to have everything at once.

His finger slipped under her bra strap. "Can I take this off?"

"Yes."

Reaching around behind her, he released the hooks. Then he slipped the straps down her arms, pulling the lacy thing aside.

Images flashed through her mind—Victor grabbing her breast, squeezing hard, pinching, fingernails digging in. Panic intruded.

"Hey, where'd you go?" Keith asked softly. His hands rested at her waist, motionless, waiting.

She took his wrist and brought his hand up to cover her breast. He kept his fingers relaxed as she drew his palm back and forth across her swollen nipple. Heat jolted through her, chasing the panic away.

Releasing his wrist, she shifted, leaning back against the pillows beside him. He continued the exquisite motion she'd started, driving her excitement higher. Then he lowered his head to her other breast, taking the sensitive tip into his mouth. As he suckled, she moaned, a long low sound.

"What do you like?" he murmured.

"Everything…everything you do."

He trailed his hand down her body to the button of her shorts. His fingers pausing there, he asked, "Okay?"

He still teased her nipple with his tongue and she could barely squeeze out her affirmation. "Yes."

Unfastening her shorts, he kneeled beside her to tug

them off. His fingers burrowed under the elastic of her bikini panties. "These, too?"

Despite the heat, despite the passion burning inside, she froze. Only for a moment, then she let go of the tension. Reaching down, she pulled the panties off herself.

Now she lay naked, vulnerable, completely at his mercy. Yet she could see only admiration in his hot gaze, desire that she knew he would hold in check as long as she asked.

Still kneeling beside her, he skimmed his hand along her body—throat, shoulder, breast, waist, hip, hesitating briefly at each destination. With each hesitation, he kissed her mouth, tongue dipping in and out so quickly, she ached for a longer exploration.

With his next kiss, she put her hand behind his neck. "If you're trying to drive me crazy with frustration, it's working."

He smiled, brushing his lips against hers. "I want to taste you…" His hand, restless on her hip, dipped between her legs. "I want to watch you climax."

The thought thrilled and terrified her. "I've never…"

One finger stroked the soft curls. "You've never had a man taste you?"

"Never—" his finger slipped between her folds and she could barely breathe "—climaxed…with a man…"

The motion of his hand ceased for an instant, then resumed its gentle friction. She could barely lie still as he slid down her body and parted her legs. But as his hands touched her inner thighs, old images returned—Victor looming over her, angry, punishing. Gasping, she pulled away, pushing up against the pillows behind her.

He stayed put, his hands still on her thighs, but relaxed and motionless. Focusing on his face, the kindness in his eyes overlaid with passion, she wiped away the ugliness, let him ease her legs apart again.

With the first touch of his tongue on her, she gasped again, but this time in exquisite pleasure. There was nothing familiar about this, the warm wetness laving her into sensation bore no resemblance to anything Victor ever did. Electricity jolted through her body with each skilled stroke, pushing her so rapidly toward a precipice, she thought she'd go out of her mind with the feelings.

She couldn't lie still. Honeyed heat flowed over her skin, leaving breathless expectation in its wake. Her fingers dug into the comforter as he nudged her closer to something she'd only dared to experience alone. She trembled on the edge, her heart slamming in her ears, the heat impossible. So ready to tip over into pleasure, something inside her resisted, still afraid.

She felt his finger lingering at her opening, drawing circles around it. She thought she'd die if he didn't push inside her, but he hesitated, teased, invading just a fraction before retreating. She knew that was the last piece of the puzzle, that she needed him inside her. His tongue, his tentative touch wasn't enough.

Groping for him, she grabbed his wrist and pulled him closer until his finger plunged inside her. She climaxed immediately, her body closing around him, a moan driven from deep inside her. She couldn't let go of him as the ecstasy washed over her in endless waves, her fingers gripping so tight she probably left bruises.

As the last shiver passed over her skin, she finally let go, falling back against the pillows, her body lax. He moved to lie alongside her, his heated gaze locking with hers. Tension came off him like sparks from a fire. Yet, she could see he held back, waiting for her cue.

"Do we stop here?" he asked, his voice raw.

It didn't surprise her that he asked, but that stopping was the last thing she wanted. In answer, her hand trailed down his body to the button of his jeans. Her fingers brushed against the dark hair that curled there as she tried to release the button, and with a sharp intake of breath, he covered her hand with his.

"Let me."

Turning away, he quickly shucked his jeans and shorts, then reached in the drawer of his bedside table. Setting a condom on the table, he lay back beside her.

She looked her fill, and her hand of its own accord reached for him. His eyes shut and he sucked in a breath when she stroked the length of him, marveling at the hardness sheathed in silk.

"This might be over before it starts," he gasped, "if you keep doing that."

Chagrined, she pulled away, but he caught her wrist to bring it to his mouth. "I'd just like to last a little longer than a heartbeat with you."

Pulling her into a loose embrace, he kissed her, his mouth warm against hers, his tongue tangling with hers. One hand covered her breast, rubbing lightly against it, rebuilding the intensity inside her. She felt wet and molten between her legs, aching for him.

But when he leaned over her, pressing her gently back, panic nibbled at her and her body tensed without conscious intention. Keith eased back again, brushing kisses across her face a moment before reaching for the foil square he'd left on the table.

She watched, fascinated, as he rolled it over himself. But he didn't move toward her again, instead lay on his back against the pillows and put out a beckoning hand.

"What do I do?" she asked, taking his hand.

"You're in control." The words were ragged. "Take me inside you."

He urged her toward him, over him, her legs straddling his hips. With her hand, she guided him to her center, then inch by slow inch, she took him inside her body.

The feeling was incredible. He filled her perfectly, seemed to touch every part of her. She could have held him like that forever.

But her body had other plans. Leaning over him so her breasts could brush against his chest, she lifted her hips, then lowered them again, slowly, then faster, then slowly again. She watched Keith's face as she moved, reveling in the power she had over his pleasure.

She leaned close enough to press her mouth to his, and his tongue plunged in and out in rhythm to the motion at the juncture of their bodies. She felt mad with sensation, on fire with it, racing for the precipice again. His hands roamed her body, teasing her breasts, skimming her hips, pulling her deeper. And it felt right, every moment of it, the fear a distant memory.

She shocked herself with a scream as she climaxed, too

crazy with sensual electricity to hold it back. He peaked moments after her, his hips lifting from the bed as he thrust inside her. Her gaze locked with his at that brilliant instant, a message in those blue eyes that caught her breath. Then the light outside shifted and whatever she'd seen there vanished.

Languorous, she shifted away from him and lay against the pillows. He climbed from the bed and walked to the master bath to clean up, returning quickly to her side. When he pulled her into his arms, her heart brimmed with emotion she didn't want to examine too closely.

His fingers toyed with her still damp hair, brushing her face with a tender caress. When she glanced up at him, he seemed troubled, and worry gnawed at Sara that the rapture she'd just experienced wasn't good enough for him.

"Was that..." She struggled to summon the right words. "Was that okay?"

He looked at her as if she was completely insane. "Okay isn't even in the same universe."

She skimmed her hand across his chest. "Then what is it?"

He didn't pretend to misunderstand. Levering himself up on one elbow, he gazed down at her. "I'm glad...very glad this was good for you." His hand curved around her face. "But this is all I can give you. A night of sex. Nothing more."

He'd warned her before. It wasn't as if he'd promised anything, or that she'd expected more. Even still, lying there, she couldn't help but feel her world was falling apart.

Chapter Thirteen

He wasn't less than honest with her. He figured he'd made it pretty clear all along that he wasn't in the market for any romantic commitments. He'd given her every chance to walk away before she got into his bed. He'd been as gentle and patient with her as he knew how to be and thought she'd enjoyed what had happened there.

So why did he feel like such a bastard?

As she worked beside him in the kitchen, cutting tomatoes for a salad, her hair tied back but still refusing to be contained, he didn't see the least reproach in her expression. She wasn't giving him the silent treatment as Melissa had done occasionally to show her displeasure with something he'd done. If anything, Sara seemed almost too neutral, as if the mind-blowing sex they'd just experienced had never happened.

If he was a different kind of man, maybe he could have manufactured some line about how much he cared for her, how important she was to him. A song and dance to make her think he loved her, happily ever after, forever and ever.

But it would have been a damn lie, when she deserved nothing but the unvarnished truth. Although he respected her, recognized that she was an incredible person, he'd had too many people torn away from him to believe in any kind of happiness, forever or otherwise.

Love had only led to pain, over and over again. He'd have to be a complete idiot to walk into that burning building again when there wasn't anything in there worth saving. Surely Sara understood that, realized she'd be better off with another man, a better man. After that SOB, Victor, she deserved happiness.

Grabbing a bag of romaine from the refrigerator, he poured half of it into the salad bowl. Their hands brushed as she dropped in the tomatoes and cucumbers, and pink streaked her cheeks, a tantalizing reminder of her responsiveness to him.

He pulled the chicken breasts from the broiler and served them up with an ear of fresh corn, handing her the plates to take to the dining-room table. He brought out the salad, tossed with a dressing she'd thrown together using olive oil, garlic and some balsamic vinegar he didn't even realize he had.

He sat next to her, serving her some salad before putting a helping on his own plate. She kept her focus on her food, cutting the boneless breast into neat bites, spreading butter on her corn on the cob. Her politeness was just about driving him crazy. He kept wondering if he should say something about what had happened in that bed, about what he'd told her. But he couldn't seem to put the words together.

She saved him the effort. "You said you had something to show me."

He had to scramble to work out what the hell she was talking about. Then he remembered and his heart squeezed in a knot. "Some pictures." He'd left them in the hallway, forgotten when he saw her after her shower, still damp and smelling of his soap. It was an entirely different fragrance on her.

"I'd like to see them." When he started to get up, she put a hand out to stop him. "After dinner. We wouldn't want to mess them up."

Settling back in his chair, he captured her hand in his. He'd had a hard enough time avoiding touching her before they'd made love. There was no way he'd be able to resist now.

He kissed her fingers, his mouth lingering against them before he released them. He'd told her one night of sex, figuring he couldn't risk taking things any further than that. But how would he keep from wanting her?

They finished their dinner in silence, Keith barely tasting the juicy chicken Sara had so carefully seasoned. Flashbacks of what had happened in the bedroom invaded his mind with every bite, and he had to make a concerted effort to keep his butt in the chair instead of dragging her off for another round.

She insisted on washing the few dishes, so he went to

retrieve the photo album he'd unearthed earlier. As he picked it up, it seemed to weigh a ton, heavy with sorrow. He hadn't flipped through the album in years, the sight of his son's smiling face too heartbreaking.

He sat on the sofa and waited for her, too afraid to open the heavy cardboard cover before he had Sara beside him. Even when she settled next to him, her sweet warmth soaking into him, he couldn't seem to open the Pandora's box.

"Can I see?" she asked, her voice so gentle, his throat suddenly felt too tight.

He set the album in her lap. She ran her fingers over the embossed lettering on the cover. Christopher Delacroix. His birth date was inscribed below that, but there was no way in hell he would write the date of his death underneath. Bad enough to see it on his headstone. Why add another nail to the coffin of guilt that consumed him?

She eased the cover open to the page filled with photos from the hospital. There was Melissa, exhausted but happy, Christopher cuddled beside her. Shots of his son alone in the bassinet, a pale blue cap on his head, his face scrunched and red. Christopher in his daddy's arms, his milky-blue eyes staring up at Keith.

Sara studied every picture. "He's so cute."

A fist thumped his chest. He had to resist the urge to yank the album from her hands, throw it back into the closet of the spare room where he kept it hidden. Pain ripped at the base of his throat, throbbing, impossible to swallow.

"Yeah," he gasped out, too lost in the agony to say more.

She turned the page to the first set of photos of Christopher at home. His son being bathed, being nursed, sleeping in his crib or howling in indignation while his diaper was changed. The sleepers his tiny body swam in at first, then grew too tight and had to be replaced. More pictures as Sara flipped through the book, Christopher crawling, standing, taking a first step.

It hurt, horribly, looking at the pictures again. He could barely breathe past the constriction in his throat, and his eyes felt wet with tears he fought with fists gripped tight in his lap. He couldn't bear much more, would have to get up and leave before he roared with the torment.

Then like a blessing, Sara's hand fell on his, stroked softly, urging away the tension. At first he didn't give in, too lost in the overwhelming emotion. But then he opened his hand and grabbed hers, a lifeline against the pain.

He squeezed his eyes shut, refusing to let go of the wetness that threatened. With his fingers laced through Sara's, he found his strength again.

He felt her kiss on his cheek, just a whisper of contact. The stricture in his throat eased, the muscles in his shoulders, at the back of his neck relaxed. He opened his eyes again.

His hand locked in Sara's, he could look at the photos again. Christopher at his first birthday party, face smeared with frosting. His son snuggled against him as he read a story about a bunny. Christopher at the San Francisco Zoo, less than a month before he died.

It still hurt terribly, but remarkably, as he saw his son's incredible smile, he smiled himself, although it barely curved his mouth. The memories the photos brought back began to soothe rather than set off that ache inside him. For the first time, a faint ember of joy glowed as he remembered his son.

Sara flipped to the last page which held a single photo. The rest of the book was empty, waiting for the recording of a lifetime that would never happen. Christopher had been sitting on the front porch, looking tired even though it was early in the day.

"He was already sick there," Keith said, his throat aching. "We didn't know." That was a lie. Melissa knew.

She traced a finger across the pinched face with its thin smile. "What was it?"

"Meningitis." He hadn't spoken the word in years. It still had an ugly sound.

He stared down at his son's small, perfect face. There had been a disposable camera in his truck that day; he used to use them to track the progress on job sites. He'd pulled it out to try to coax a smile from Christopher. It ended up being their last picture of him.

"Melissa called me in a panic from the emergency room. I drove like a madman to get there. He hung on, as if he knew I had to say goodbye…"

His son, his body filled with tubes and wires, too small in the intensive care bed. That image had jammed itself in his brain, too vivid to ignore, too unbearable to recall. Remembering brought back the guilt, tore him up so much he couldn't function. So he'd plastered over the memory, built a wall around it more impenetrable than cinderblock and concrete.

The anchor of Sara's hand pulled him back from that jagged abyss. She set the album aside and put her arms around him, resting her head on his shoulder. Emotion still banged around inside him, exposing him to a vulnerability he couldn't surrender to.

He knew one sure distraction, and she sat there in his arms, her body more powerful than the pain. Shifting her, he pressed his mouth to hers, sweeping his tongue inside, tasting her wet heat. Tugging at the elastic band holding her hair back, he pulled it loose, freeing her glorious hair.

Their lovemaking before should have dulled the intensity of his reaction to her, the mystery of that first time solved. But new mysteries spun themselves, with new places to touch, new ways too incite her passions. He burned to watch her climax again, to feel her body closing around his, pulsing in release.

With another woman, he might have gone as quickly as his body demanded, pulling off the T-shirt that looked a damned sight better on her than him, unzipping her shorts, slipping his fingers inside her panties. Another woman might have welcomed the rush, the impatience to come together.

But this was Sara. Sara who'd been treated so badly in her life, Sara who deserved a perfect lover, not an angry, flawed man like him. But while he couldn't refuse the gift of her in his arms, he could do everything he could to keep her feeling safe.

Stretching out on the sofa, he pulled her over him, the sweet weight of her body a tantalizing pleasure. Her breasts against his chest stole his breath. Her mouth, hot and welcoming as he explored inside with his tongue, sharpened the edge of his desire.

He thrust up with his hips, instinct compelling him to get even closer to her. In response, she brought one knee up, fitting herself against him. Feeling his hard length pressed into her softness, he thought he'd explode.

She drew back, grabbing handfuls of his T-shirt, dragging it up his body. As he yanked it off and threw it aside, she sat up, her center grinding into him, pounding sensation through him. As he struggled for the willpower to hold back, she slowly took off her own shirt, the color along her cheeks telling him she still felt shy about it.

Her breasts seemed to strain at the bra, begged him to touch. Moving his hands along her thighs, her waist, up her rib cage, he watched her face, searching for any signal telling him to stop. But when his hands hesitated just below her bra, she took them, cupping them over her breasts, a blatant invitation.

He skimmed his palms over the plain white knit, felt her nipples bead as he stroked her. He urged her closer, then put his mouth where his hand had been and nipped gently with his teeth. She gasped, her fingers tightening on his shoulders.

Reaching behind her, he unfastened the hooks of her bra, then eased the straps down her arms. As she took in a shuddering breath, her breasts lifted, the tips deep rose and luscious.

Arching up, he circled one nipple with his tongue, his fingers teasing the other. She moaned, and he could feel the reflexive response between her legs where she pressed against him. He wondered if he could bring her to climax just from touching her, licking her. It seemed a miracle that despite her fears, despite the horrors in her life, she could be so responsive.

All the more reason to give her every bit of pleasure he could. To find exactly what she liked, how she liked it. Draw out the sensations. Give her every part of himself that he could.

His hands, his mouth, his tongue. The aching part of his body that he longed to slip deep inside her, to bring his own completion. Everything physical he could give her without hesitation.

But nothing deeper. Not his heart—there was nothing there anymore but hollowness and loneliness. Not his emotions—they were black and absent. And love—if that had ever existed for him, too many deaths had blotted it out forever.

So there was only this—Sara's breast resting heavy in his hand, her nipple against his tongue, his lips pleasuring her. Later, he would taste her as he had earlier, bring her to a mind-numbing climax, then pour himself into her. The physical would have to be enough. For both of them.

He nipped again, dragging his teeth lightly on that sensitive tip and she threw her head back, squirming against him. The sudden pressure nearly stripped away his precarious self-control, her heat almost impossible to resist.

For an instant, he wanted to shove down his jeans and her shorts, pull her onto him, plunge deep inside her. He knew she'd climax immediately, could feel how close to the edge she was. Her wet heat would be heaven, would bring him as quickly to that paradise.

It would be so easy, even with the care he had to take with her. Just a matter of buttons and zippers, the miniscule scrap of her panties, his shorts. Her body would welcome his, surround his.

His hand moved to the button on her shorts just as hers reached for the waistband of his jeans. Her fingers brushing against his belly, fumbling with his fly, nearly blew his mind. He thrust up against her, impossibly close, his body ready and anticipating the culmination it craved.

He had her zipper down and she'd nearly done the same with his jeans when realization hit him like a ten ton boulder. *He didn't have protection.* He'd been ready and willing to plunge inside her, to bring them both to climax without a condom. Risk pregnancy, risk changing both their lives.

Pushing her hand aside, he levered himself up, then rose with her in his arms. Caught by surprise, she grabbed his shoulders, tense and worried. He brushed a kiss across her brow as he headed down the hall and she relaxed again, softening under his mouth's caress.

"Protection," he whispered. "In the bedroom."

He laid her on the bed and reached in the drawer. Then he pushed off his jeans as she kicked off her shorts and panties. He rolled the condom over himself and lowered himself to the bed.

She lay back, arms open, legs apart and welcoming. "I want to try this," she murmured.

Kneeling between her legs, he leaned over her. "Take me inside."

Her hand around him drove thought clean from his head. She guided him closer, tipped her hips toward him as he entered slowly. He lowered himself, resting on his elbows to save her from his weight.

Fully inside her, he held tight to his control. "Okay?"

She wrapped her arms around his shoulders, her legs around his hips. "Very okay."

He moved, keeping his thrusts slow and easy, watching her face every moment, alert for any uncertainty. But he saw only passion, building, growing, her mouth growing fuller and more lush with each kiss, her breasts hot against his chest.

He didn't know how he kept from his own climax before she reached hers; it was a near thing. The first tightening of her muscles around him tipped the scales, launching him into a dizzying ecstasy. Her moans rang in his ears, adding to the sensations, breaking his world apart before it settled again in an entirely different configuration.

Easing his body to one side, he held her tightly in his arms, breathing her sweet fragrance, indulging in her warm softness. If he could, he would lie here forever.

Her breathing steadied as she fell asleep beside him, her silky hair draped across his chest. As he half dozed, every nerve in his body still singing in the aftermath, the boulder that had hit him earlier swung back and struck him again.

Maybe it wouldn't have been so bad if he'd forgotten the condom.

He couldn't believe his own arrogance. He didn't deserve another child, certainly not Sara's. His neglect had led to his own son's death.

And yet...the thought of his baby inside her, a new start, a fresh chance, threatened to melt the ice encasing his heart. The temptation to give in whispered to him.

He'd squandered that chance with his son. He had no right to another. It was enough that he had Sara in his arms, her sweetness a temporary balm against the pain. He damn well wouldn't ask for anything more.

Sara woke with a start, panicking momentarily at the feel of Keith's arms around her. In that instant, it was Victor holding her down, preventing her escape. She wrenched free, slid to the other side of the bed...then she remembered where she was and who she was with.

He slept so deeply, he hadn't even stirred, despite her struggles. Feeling badly that she'd mistaken Keith for Victor, even in her semiconscious state, she stroked his arm in silent apology. He let out a long, relaxed breath, then seemed to settle even more deeply into sleep.

Her heart felt as if it would burst. The last several hours had been beyond anything she thought she would ever experience. He'd given her a monumental gift—control of her body and its pleasure. He'd made her feel sensual and sexy and womanly...and loved.

Only physically. He'd told her he couldn't give her anything more than that. It should have been enough.

Would have been enough. If she hadn't been so stupid as to read more into the emotions swirling inside her. Given them names she shouldn't, told herself lies. That what she felt for him wasn't just affection, wasn't just passion. That it was more.

A sliver of a crescent moon barely chased the darkness, painting his incredible body with shadows. His muscles honed by years of hard work, his hands rough with two decades of wielding hammer and saws, toting and hewing lumber, he nevertheless had been tender and kind and caring. He'd been patient with her fears, given her far more than she'd given him.

No wonder she thought she loved him.

She slipped from the bed and searched in the near darkness for her shorts. The bedside clock told her it was nearly 2:00 a.m. She'd slept solidly for over five hours. A testament to how safe she felt with him; she usually tossed and turned, two hour stretches of sleep interspersed with restless waking.

She padded down the hall for the rest of her clothes. They'd left the kitchen light on, which made it easy to find her bra and the T-shirt he'd lent her. She ought to just retrieve her tank top and leave his here, but once she'd pulled the T-shirt on, the soft knit caressing her body as his hands had, she couldn't bring herself to take it off again. She'd just wear it home, return it later.

The photo album still lay open to the photo of Keith's son, Christopher. His grief over his son's death had been palpable, seemed so deep she wondered if it would ever heal. She longed to find the right words, the correct sentiment to take away the pain. But despite all her education, her experience as a counselor, she felt completely incompetent.

As she stepped out the front door, a herd of deer strolled across the front yard, quickening their pace when they spied her. Beyond them, slinking across a field alongside the house, a coyote made its lonely way. Above, a meteor slashed across the field of stars, leaving a comet trail of light.

Had Keith ever woken his son in the middle of the night, brought him outside to watch falling stars? Sara had a dim memory of her mother rousing her on a black, moonless night and taking her into the backyard. A blanket spread on the damp grass, they had lain there for hours staring up at the stars. It had been a paltry showing there in the city, unlike the extravagance of this rural display. But lying beside her mother, holding her hand, it wouldn't have mattered if it had been an empty sky.

As Sara started her engine, a light flickered on in Keith's house, at the far end where his bedroom was located. At the least, he knew she'd left his bed. If he made the effort of looking through his house, he'd realize she'd gone entirely. She ought to pull away, get out of here before he saw her.

She put the car in gear, but her foot remained on the brake. It was ridiculous to wait, wouldn't change a thing if she saw his face. But she couldn't seem to move her foot to the accelerator.

He opened the door, stepped out onto the porch, in his jeans but shirtless. Moving to the edge of the porch, he turned toward her car, stared at the windshield, although he couldn't possibly see her through the headlights' glare. Just stood there, watching, one hand gripping the balustrade.

Did he want her to come back inside? If she did, they'd

certainly make love again. He'd send her back into that bliss, give her the glory of his body. She could pretend to be satisfied with that.

She could pretend he wanted something more. Fool herself into believing he'd come out here to bring her back because he felt more than passion for her. If he'd just take a step closer, come down the stairs toward her, maybe she could persuade herself to believe it.

He didn't move.

She eased her foot from the brake, backed her car in an arc. She took one last look at him in her rearview mirror as she drove away, although without the headlights' illumination, she couldn't be sure he was still there on the porch.

But she could imagine him all too clearly, his grief a cloak of pain, loneliness filling his world.

Chapter Fourteen

June dragged into July, the temperatures rising into triple digits, forcing the camp day to start an hour earlier so they could finish before the heat grew unbearable. Grace returned to camp, thanks again to Jameson paying her way and due to Dani's sister's return from college. Home for the summer, nineteen-year-old Rachael was more than happy to make a little money transporting Grace to and from the ranch.

Three weeks had passed since the day of the picnic, since Sara's night with Keith. Whether by design or happenstance, he'd stayed away, not even showing his face when the irrigation man came to run the plumbing for the wash rack. They hadn't crossed paths in town, either, at least not in Hart Valley. Once or twice she'd caught a glimpse of a Delacroix Construction truck, but it had been too far away to see who was driving.

He owed her nothing. His commitment to the program, to Grace, was finished. The completed barn provided the horses shade in the brutal afternoon heat, and the wash rack gave her a place to cool them after each day's workout. She didn't have the right to ask Keith for anything more.

Standing in the blessed coolness of her kitchen, a glass of iced tea chilling her hands, Sara stared out the window at the wash rack where Grace and Dani were giving Dudley a thorough bath. After the breakthrough on the day of the picnic and three more weeks of camp, Grace had morphed into an entirely different little girl. She chattered like a magpie now, as if she had to make up for all those months of silence. She smiled often, the joy reaching her eyes as it never had before.

Not even Dudley's imminent departure from the ranch could dull Grace's happiness. Once Sara promised the little girl she could accompany her and Tom Jarret over to the Double J, Grace responded with excitement instead of sorrow. It had been her idea to bathe Dudley, to make sure the old horse sparkled when he met his new friends at the Jarrets's ranch.

Tom would be here within the hour to haul the elderly gelding to his retirement home. It had taken a full three weeks to coordinate the move, between Tom's busy schedule and hers. They had a narrow window this afternoon, since Tom and Andrea were heading to South Lake Tahoe for the weekend and they wanted to beat the Friday evening traffic.

Outside, Grace and Dani gave Dudley a last rinse and ran the sweat scraper over his coat to shed the excess water. Dudley shook his big body, spraying Grace and Dani. Grace laughed uproariously, collapsing to the grass edging the wash rack, wiping away the wetness on her face. Sara's heart filled at the miracle she was witnessing.

She should have been over the moon with happiness at her success with Grace. But that triumph, as marvelous as it was, couldn't soothe the constant longing Sara felt for Keith. Some mornings, especially after having a nightmare, she had to struggle to drag herself out of bed. With reminders of him all around, the T-shirt she wore every night to bed, the barn and wash rack that he had built, she couldn't banish him from her mind, despite every effort.

Because she loved him. All the mental lectures in the world, scolding herself about how impossible, how impractical it was, hadn't extinguished that powerful emotion.

Meeting Keith had been a blessing. She'd learned that what she'd felt for Victor hadn't even been the palest imitation of real love. It healed her to know she could fall in love with a good man, and she hadn't truly given her heart to a bad one.

Keith had also shown her she could experience physical pleasure, had opened her body to the possibilities of passion. It was a wasted lesson in a way—she couldn't imagine herself with another man—but it repaired some of the worst of Victor's emotional damage.

She glanced up at the kitchen clock. Nearly three. She'd ended camp early at two, had made sure all the kids cleared out of here quickly so she could get Dudley loaded the moment Tom showed up. But still no Tom.

Grabbing her address book to look up Tom's number, she saw the newspaper clipping, still tucked inside. Pulling it out and studying it for probably the thousandth time, she decided she wasn't going to let her father haunt her anymore. The photo was doubtless of some other man anyway, not worth an ounce of her worry.

Tearing it in two, she dropped it in the trash just as the sound of a diesel engine announced Tom Jarret's arrival. Downing the rest of her iced tea, she hurried back to her office for her tote bag, then started for the door. She'd pulled her hatchback out into the parking area already, intending to follow Tom in her car with Grace.

The truck and trailer had already turned toward the exit by the time she reached the parking area. The two-horse rig, emblazoned with the Double J logo, blocked her view of the truck, so she couldn't see whether Tom had brought Andrea or his daughter Jessie with him.

Rounding the back of the trailer, she stopped short when she got a good look at the pickup and the Delacroix Construction sign on the side. As she tried to figure out why Tom Jarret would have borrowed Keith's truck, the door opened and Keith stepped out onto the gravel.

He walked slowly toward her. "Hello, Sara."

She thrust aside the joy bubbling up inside her, angry at her hopeless reaction. "What are you doing here?"

"One of Tom's brood mares cut herself in the pasture. He had to get the vet out."

"He didn't call."

"He called me instead. I had the afternoon free." He stood near enough to touch now. "How have you been, Sara?"

Aching. Heartbroken. Wanting you so badly I can't sleep or eat.

But she wasn't about to reveal the truth. "I've been fine."

He stared down at her, a hunger in his face she didn't want to see. Because it only fed her own.

An arm's length apart, they walked around the trailer toward the wash rack where Dudley dozed in the sun. Dani and Grace sat at the picnic table, munching chips and slurping juice boxes.

Dani stood up. "Gotta go." Tossing her trash on the way, she headed toward her car.

"Hi, Uncle Keith!" Grace gave him an enthusiastic hug.

Sara wished it could be as easy for her. That she could just walk over to Keith, put her arms around him, feel him hold her close. If wishes were horses… Hooking her tote bag over her shoulder, she untied Dudley's lead rope and led him toward the trailer as Keith and Grace followed. She could feel his gaze on her, but she didn't dare look back.

Once they had the gelding secure in the trailer, she took Grace's hand. "We'll follow you in my car."

Grace bounced with excitement. "I want to ride with Uncle Keith and Dudley."

Keith's blue eyes fixed on Sara. "You should both go with me. I come back this way anyway."

For her own sanity, she ought to say no. But she couldn't bring herself to pass up the chance to spend a few minutes with him, as foolhardy as that might be.

Opening the truck's passenger side door, Sara stood back to let Grace sit in the middle of the bench seat. The little girl hung back. "Can I sit by the window? Then I can watch the trailer in the mirror. Make sure Dudley's okay."

Which meant Sara would be crammed against Keith, so close it would be impossible to keep from touching him. But she couldn't deny the little girl such a small favor.

Sara settled next to him, Grace by the window with her gaze riveted on the side view mirror. Sara tried to keep space between her and Keith, but with the first right turn onto Stony Creek Road, her arm brushed his, skin grazing skin. Her thigh slid alongside his and a myriad of erotic memories flooded her.

She'd be a basket case by the time they traveled the five or six miles over to the Jarrets's ranch. A glance up at him told her he wasn't immune to the contact; his jaw flexed and his hands held the wheel in a death grip.

Desperate for a distraction, she jumped on the first thing that came to mind. "Did Jameson tell you about the fund-raising dance next Saturday? We've got a country western band from Reno coming in. Jameson's renting a dance floor for the covered arena."

"I can't come."

Disappointment bit at her as he lapsed into silence, his body far too close, his heart and soul a million miles away. She wanted so badly to lean against him, rest her head on his shoulder. But that would only make her feel worse when he left again.

He slowed as he drove over a narrow bridge, then turned onto the road that fronted the Jarrets's ranch. He shifted into a lower gear as the truck took the incline of the rutted gravel driveway leading to the house, the engine roaring with the effort. Pine and oak branches slapped the sides of the truck and trailer as they made their way through the trees.

One last turn, then they arrived on the sun-drenched hilltop with its white clapboard farmhouse, big red barn and corrals. Renowned in the cutting and reining world for the quarter horses he bred and trained, Tom would give Dudley an excellent home. The old gelding would likely be an uncle to the foals at weaning time.

Keith pulled the rig clear of the vet's truck, which was parked over by the barn. Dr. Samuel Fox, the vet who volunteered at the Rescued Hearts program, was just wrapping a bandage around the front left leg of a sorrel mare. Beside Dr. Fox, Tom waved as he handed the vet another roll of bandage.

Grace rocketed out of the pickup as Andrea started down the porch steps toward them. "Hi, Mrs. Jarret!" She gave her former teacher a lavish hug.

Andrea held Grace's hand as they walked to the rear of the trailer.

Andrea and Grace put the chestnut gelding into a paddock of his own, surrounded by mares and foals, to give him a chance to get acquainted. Leaving the horse munching grass hay under the shade of a massive oak, they headed for the front porch where Andrea's eleven-year-old stepdaughter, Jessie, had brought out a pitcher of lemonade on a tray.

Jessie handed out the filled glasses. "Did you tell her?"

"Not yet, sweetheart." Andrea smiled at Sara. "I've already called Alicia. If Grace likes, she can spend the rest of the afternoon here, to make sure Dudley gets settled. I'll take her home after dinner."

"Yes!" Grace responded immediately. "Yes, yes, yes!"

Jessie set her lemonade glass down with a clunk, then plucked Grace's half-finished tumbler from the little girl's hands. "Come on, I'll show you the foals." The two girls pounded down the porch steps, then across the yard toward the pasture.

Keith downed the rest of his drink, the movement of his throat intriguing and enticing. When he lowered the glass, he caught Sara watching him. His blue eyes burned into her and she thought she might melt on the spot.

He dropped his glass on the tray with a clatter and started down the steps toward the truck. "I'll get the trailer unhitched."

Sara couldn't seem to tear her gaze away from him as he strode across the dusty yard. The three weeks without him had seemed to stretch forever. After today, how much longer before she saw him again? How long before she could stop aching for him every day?

She heard Andrea's low chuckle. "I didn't know there was something going on with you and Keith."

Alarmed, Sara spilled lemonade on her hand. "We aren't. There isn't."

"The last time I saw so many fireworks was when I first met Tom." She cast a loving glance over at her husband. "We didn't know what hit us."

Tom lifted his gaze to Andrea's, his slow smile telling

Sara just how much he adored his wife. Sara longed for that kind of adoration.

Turning to where Keith backed the two-horse next to a bigger rig, she tried to push aside the welling emotion. What would it be like if Keith felt that same love for her? If their lives were as inextricably linked as Tom's and Andrea's? It would be forever, because if Keith committed to her, he wouldn't offer her anything less than always.

Except he hadn't committed to her, he wouldn't. Because he didn't love her.

Andrea touched her arm softly. "Does he know?"

Sara eased away from Andrea. "There's nothing to know. Nothing I want him to know."

The relentless pain pounded inside her as Keith walked toward them. "Are you ready?"

Sara set aside her untouched glass of lemonade. "Thanks for everything, Andrea. I'll call in a few days to see how Dudley's doing."

She climbed into the truck, grateful to have the space between her and Keith on the bench seat. As they made their slow way back down the steep driveway, she glanced over at Keith. He seemed just as tightly wound as he'd been on the drive over, his fingers still strangling the steering wheel.

Sara angled toward him. "Why did you do this?"

"Do what?"

She tamped down her irritation. "Why did you agree to pick up Dudley?"

"Just trying to help."

"You've stayed away for three solid weeks. Not a call. Not a word from you."

He shrugged, but the tightness in his shoulders gave away his tension. "You didn't need me."

Pain knotted in her chest. "No, I guess I didn't." The lie sat bitterly on her tongue.

He turned onto the rutted road that fronted the Jarrets's ranch. "I didn't promise you anything."

Trees and fence posts passed the window in a blur. "You didn't."

"I have nothing to give you, Sara."

He had so much to give. He just wasn't willing to give it to her. "I wish you hadn't come."

The words dropped like pebbles in a pond, concentric circles of hurt encompassing them both. Keith sailed right past the turn toward Stony Creek Road, but Sara felt too heartsick to point it out to him. He'd figure it out soon enough on his own.

He kept driving, the silence beating out its measure in the truck cab. He turned on another narrow country road, but instead of making a U-turn back the way they came, he kept going. At the first intersection, he turned left, then wound his way through the trees, occasionally turning left or right, whether aimlessly or with a destination in mind, Sara didn't know.

Eventually, he pulled up to the entrance of Deer Creek Campground and followed an SUV full of teenagers inside. After a stop at the kiosk to pay a user fee, he made his way slowly along the access road, finally stopping in front of space number 312.

A family was just setting up in the adjoining lot, but as Keith climbed from the truck and started off into the trees, he didn't so much as look their way. After a moment's hesitation, Sara quickly followed him, waving at the young mother passing out snacks to her two preschoolers as her husband and older daughter set up the tent.

She caught up to Keith at the creek. As hot as the summer had been, the creek's level had dropped far below the bank, the rushing flood of spring gone. Keith sat on a wide boulder, his feet at the water's edge, head bowed.

Sara lowered herself beside him, longing to throw her arms around his rigid shoulders. But what was the point when he wouldn't let her inside?

He heaved in a long breath, staring down at the creek. He had to know she was there, but he might as well have been on another planet. A bubble of pain seemed to surround him, an impervious shell to keep the hurt inside.

Then he fumbled for her hand, and she thought her heart would burst. When she ought to be walking away from him out of self-preservation, she felt compelled to offer him what comfort she could.

His fingers clenched around hers. "There wasn't enough time." His throat sounded raw. "Two years—it was nothing. But it was all I got."

"With Christopher?"

"I thought I'd bring him camping." His other hand swallowed hers. "Catch a few fish, roast a few marshmallows."

She didn't know what to do but hang onto him. "You never brought him here?"

"Once." He took in a labored breath. "Melissa brought him to the work site for lunch. We ate here, by the water. He was…twenty months, maybe? A handful and a half.

Melissa just about had a heart attack when he tried to jump in the creek."

She could imagine that towhead boy with mischievous blue eyes and a rakish grin, looking for fishies in the rushing creek. All her training as a counselor and she could think of nothing but platitudes—life goes on, you have your memories of him. The only thing she knew was right in that moment was to hold his hand, impart what strength to him she could.

After a while, the noise of the young family filtered through the trees as they made their way to the creek. Keith shifted and rose, helping her up the bank, avoiding even the least sideways glance at the three-year-old boy that walked toward them with his mother. He held her hand tighter as the boy passed, his body taut with strain.

At the truck, he opened her door and helped her inside, then when he climbed in himself, he reached for her. "Sit beside me. Please."

She undid her seat belt, then slid over to the middle. He turned the truck around, his arm brushing hers as he maneuvered. Once they'd left the campground and returned to the county road, he took her hand, holding it against his thigh.

As they drove to the NJN Ranch, she'd struggled against the physical sensations sitting next to him. Now, she felt only her love for him, the longing to make things right, to somehow heal the pain inside him. She couldn't. Not unless he let her in, and that was never going to happen.

When they pulled into Sara's driveway, he parked the

truck near her house, but he didn't shut off the engine. He still held tight to her hand.

"Did you want to come in?" she asked.

"We'll end up in your bed if I do."

"I know."

His steady gaze locked with hers. "That's as far as it'll go. Nothing's changed, Sara."

She clamped down on the surge of emotion, groped for the truck's door handle. She had it open, was about to step down.

"Sara, I'm leaving."

Don't look back! But she did. "Leaving…?"

"I'm going to Reno. To help out at my brother's construction company for a while."

"How long?" she asked, not wanting to hear the answer.

"I don't know. I spent the last three weeks tying up loose ends here."

"But you'll be back."

Her heart sank at his long hesitation. "I think it might be time to move on." He cleared his throat. "There's nothing here for me anymore."

He might as well have plunged a lance in her chest. Tearing away, she pushed out of the truck, then ran to the house without looking back.

As she unlocked her door, she heard the rumble of the engine as he drove away. She got as far as the living room before she collapsed, sobbing, on the couch.

Chapter Fifteen

Saturday night, with close to a hundred and fifty people milling about the NJN Ranch, Sara sat alone at one of the dozen picnic tables set up at one end of the covered arena, nursing a glass of iced tea. She couldn't quite get comfortable in the stiff new jeans she wore in honor of the party. At ten past nine, she felt too warm in the still sultry air, and her Rescued Hearts T-shirt clung damply to her back.

The dance floor was empty for the moment as the band took a break. The buffet set up in the barn aisle, provided by Nina's Café, was nearly eaten to the last scrap. The horses, dozing out in their paddocks, were probably about ready to burst from all the carrots they'd been offered.

Jameson's fund-raiser was a smashing success by any measure. He'd invited Sacramento and Bay Area industry titans like Lucas Taylor of TaylorMade Foods and Richard Hightower from Hightower National Networks. He'd also included local Marbleville County business owners as well as ordinary Hart Valley citizens.

Every one of them had pulled out their checkbooks to donate to the program. Rescued Hearts now had enough funding to set up scholarships, to build an outdoor jumping arena and start on the addition to the house, and to bring in a second counselor when the need arose.

Sara should have been thrilled. She was, truly, once she dug under all those layers of despair that had closed around her this past week. A nugget of joy lay deep inside that the program and the children she cared for so much would be continuing and expanding.

The country western band Jameson had brought down from Reno made their way back to the stage set up at the other end of the arena. The dance floor, laid out on the soft arena footing, filled quickly as couples wandered over in anticipation of the music. Sara wondered how soon she could slip away to her little house. Last time she checked, Jameson's wife Nina was collecting donations at Sara's dinette table.

Jameson sat talking with a garrulous group of businessmen at another table, looking pretty darn convincing in his Western shirt and boots despite never having been on a horse. He caught her eye, then excused himself and headed her way.

As much as she liked her boss and appreciated what he'd done for the program, Sara wasn't really up for a conversation. Still, she forced a smile as he approached. "You done good, boss."

His grin crinkled the corners of his blue eyes as he sat beside her. "Your work is what convinced them. The results you've gotten. That and Grace charming the socks off them."

The little girl had put in an appearance with her mother earlier in the evening. She'd personally taken the strait-laced businessmen and women on guided tours of the ranch, describing each horse in excruciating detail.

Sara took another sip of her tea to mask a sigh. Jameson, too observant by half, narrowed his piercing gaze on her. "I thought he'd be here," he said gently.

Her throat tightened. "Who?"

"I think you know."

She laughed, but there wasn't much joy in it. "Have you been listening to the Hart Valley busybodies?"

He shrugged his broad shoulders. "Andrea Jarret is a good friend of Nina's. They indulged in a little gossip at the café and I overheard."

"There truly is nothing between us, Jameson." At least nothing reciprocal. "Keith and I don't make for very juicy gossip."

"He's a good man, Sara."

"That was never in doubt."

Jameson leaned closer. "He could use a good woman."

Sara took another sip of tea, but she could barely swallow. "He left, Jameson."

"Yeah." He looked up as someone walked toward them. "Did I introduce my attorney friend, John Evans? He's from Sacramento."

John flashed a perfect smile as he shook her hand. "So

this is the miracle worker. Do you suppose I could drag you onto the dance floor?"

She wanted to crawl into bed and pull the covers over her head. But she thought she could make nice with one more potential donor. "I'd love to."

The band segued into a Garth Brooks song about how missing life's pain meant missing life's dance. She'd had that dance with Keith, that moment in his arms. It was over, but wasn't it better to have had that chance with him?

As they moved across the floor, John held her with decorum, not so close as to set off her panic. Nearby, Jameson danced with his wife, Nina, in a tight embrace. If Nina was out here, it meant Sara's house was empty and after she excused herself from John, she could go to bed.

He gazed down at her, his brown eyes bright with intelligence. "I'm incredibly impressed with what you've done here."

Before she could frame a response, the roar of an approaching car snagged her attention. A vehicle pulled into the driveway, its glaring headlights strafing the arena as it parked. It was nearly ten. Who could be getting here so late?

John turned her away from the parking area and the closely packed bodies hid the new arrival from view. The song was nearing the end, its bittersweet melancholy setting off a pang inside Sara.

Then the crowd shifted as someone cut through the dance floor. A hand fell on John's shoulder—Keith's hand. He stood there, his expression stormy, his grip implacable. "She's dancing with me now."

John yanked away, blocking Sara from Keith with his body. "Who the hell are you?"

Sara's heart pounded in her ears. "I'm sorry," she said to John. "If you could excuse us."

"Sure. If you're okay." She nodded, never taking her eyes from Keith as John headed off the dance floor.

The Garth Brooks song ended and the band picked up a lively tune. Keith stood there, staring at her as couples two-stepped around them.

She took his hand and led him away from the crowd, across the arena, out the gate. She knew she could let go and he'd follow, but she wanted the connection with him as long as she could have it, the warmth of his skin against hers.

She took him inside her house, letting go of him to close and lock the door behind her. When she turned back to him, he was pacing her living room floor, energy coming off him in waves.

Facing her, he scraped a hand through his hair. "I don't know why I'm here."

She wanted the reason to be because he had to be with her. But that was just wishful thinking. "I thought you were in Reno."

He seemed shrouded in an unnamable sadness. "I was."

Something was brewing inside him; she could see it fighting its way to the surface. But she hadn't a clue how to help him, or if she even should. "Why did you come back?"

There was a wild look of grief in his eyes. "I couldn't stay away. I had to be here. Tonight."

She didn't know what he'd do if she touched him, if

he'd flinch away from her or move into the contact. Nevertheless, she felt compelled to try.

Stepping closer, she curved her hand around his cheek. "What's special about tonight?"

"It's the anniversary," he rasped out. He glanced at her kitchen clock, his beard rasping against her palm. "Ten forty-eight. Forty-three minutes from now."

Confusion gave way to understanding. "That's when Christopher died?"

He dragged in a breath. "Yes. Six years…" Stumbling backward, he sank onto the sofa. "God, it hurts. I can't stop it hurting." He dropped his head in his hands.

Sara sat close beside him, her arm around his waist. "Talk to me, Keith."

Dropping his hands, he took another shuddering breath. "Since I met you, everything's been…crazy inside."

She stroked his back. "I'm sorry."

"It's not anything that's your fault." He shook his head. "It's just…I thought I had it all behind me. The grief. The guilt."

"Because your son died?"

"Because I'm to blame." Grabbing her hand, he held it tight. "When Melissa called me that day Christopher was sick, I told her not to worry. That it was only a cold or the flu."

She squeezed his hand. "You didn't know."

"She waited to take him." His body spasmed as if in reaction to severe pain. "She waited until he was so ill…they couldn't help him…couldn't bring him back…too late to save him…all because…because I…"

Bent over, he curled tight into himself as if it would keep the agony inside. Sara just hung on, holding his hand, stroking his back. "You didn't know," she whispered. "You didn't know."

Then the dam broke, sobs pouring from him, wrenched from deep inside. She wondered if he'd ever cried for his son, or if his guilt had shut down even that intense emotion. He probably felt he didn't deserve the tears because he couldn't save his son's life.

She stayed close to him, soaking up his grief, whispering whatever comfort came into her mind to say. If he heard any of it, she didn't know, but after a long while, he grew peaceful, quiet.

His wet gaze strayed to the clock again. Sara's did as well. It wasn't much longer.

Their fingers interlaced, they watched the hands of the clock move minute by minute as they approached the hour of Christopher's death. When the time ticked into place, another shudder passed through Keith's body.

"Goodbye, Christopher. I love you, son."

Then the clock moved on. Keith pulled her onto his lap and into his arms, pressing a kiss into her hair. "This is your fault, you know." The words came out rough, but laced with humor.

She pulled back. "What do you mean?"

She saw a yearning in his face she didn't dare interpret. He tucked a strand of hair behind her ear. "Because you made me feel again."

Hope fluttered in her chest, struggled to get free. She cradled his face with her hands. "Feel what?"

"Love, sweetheart." His clear blue gaze met hers, steady, sure. "Love."

An explosion of joy burst inside, but she was still afraid to let herself believe. She tried to see the truth in his face, in his eyes.

He trailed a finger gently down her cheek. "I love you, Sara. I've run away from that fact for weeks now. I can't run anymore."

Tears welled in her eyes and she let them fall. "I love you, Keith. So very much."

He smiled, slowly, and it seemed as if the sun had risen in the middle of the night. "I'm damn glad of that."

He kissed her, his mouth warm and urgent against hers. Pulling her T-shirt free of her jeans, he dove underneath to cup her breast. His palm brushing against her nipple sent instant sensation through her.

She squirmed against him, knowing what his reaction would be, reveling in it. His groan vibrated through her, intensifying the heat building inside her.

His hand was restless against her breast. "I want you, Sara. So badly."

"Please…" was all she could manage.

He lifted her in his arms and headed toward her bedroom. He lay her on her bed, started to stretch out beside her.

She stopped him. "The window."

He looked back over his shoulder as the curtain drifted inward from a light breeze. "You don't want to hear the music while we make love?"

"I'd rather they don't hear me." She smiled. "I plan to be noisy."

He laughed, a beautiful sound, and she thought she couldn't be any happier. "I'll hold you to that," he said as he shut the window.

She held out her arms to him and he lay beside her. Between kisses and caresses, they pulled off jeans and T-shirts, his shorts, her panties and bra. She was so eager to take him inside, she curled her hand around him as she spread her legs.

"Wait," he gasped out. He tugged her hand away, brought it up for a kiss before he slid from the bed to grab his jeans. He pulled a condom from his wallet and sheathed himself.

This time when she took him, he let her guide him inside, his body over hers. She pulled him down toward her, wanting to feel the weight of his body, secure and so very safe with him.

As he thrust inside her, the sensations spiraled higher, pushing her to the edge, closer, closer. His mouth on hers, his tongue dueling with hers, the firm muscles of his chest against her breasts—it all overwhelmed her. Knowing she loved him, that he loved her, heightened every emotion, every spark of electricity running along her nerves.

Just when she thought she would scream from the intensity, her climax hit, driving a moan from her body. He thrust more deeply and she peaked again, nearly in tears from the exquisiteness of it. Then she held him as he reached his own climax, as he roared out her name.

His body blanketed hers, skin against skin, the heat soaking into her. Only the slightest shift and he eased from her to lie by her side. She laid there, listening to his breathing, reveling in his presence.

He kissed her brow. "Marry me."

She arched her neck so she could look into his eyes. They were half-lidded, drowsy with satisfaction. "Are you sure?"

"Yes." Another soft press of his mouth. "Completely. Totally. Certain to my bones."

"Then, yes."

His mouth curled up in a smile, but the faintest worry lurked in his eyes. "Are you sure?"

It was beyond what she'd ever hoped for in her life. To have a man like Keith at her side, to protect her, to love her. "Very, very sure."

Grinning, he went up on one elbow and trailed a finger down between her breasts. "I think I saw Reverend Pennington out there. We could take care of it right now."

She couldn't hold back an answering smile. "I think he might insist on a license."

Keith sighed, lying back. "Guess so. Tomorrow, then."

Sara laughed, then a realization bubbling up inside sobered her. "Keith."

He'd closed his eyes completely. "Yes?"

She wrestled with the right words. "Would you be willing to try again? To have another child?"

Tension seized his body for a moment, then subsided. He lifted on his elbow again. "I can't ever bring him back."

"No."

"But a brother…or a sister…" His voice grew ragged, but he smiled. "With you. Your child. Yes."

"Our child," she said and threw her arms around him. "I love you, Keith."

"I love you," he said, emotion strengthening the words. "I love you, forever."

Epilogue

Pulling their brand-new four-door sedan as close as he could to his house, Keith took a quick glance at the baby seat in the back before opening the car door. "Don't move," he told Sara when she started to open her own door.

He hurried around to her side, taking her hand to ease her exit from the car. She winced as she straightened. "Darn C-section."

Once he was sure she was steady on her feet, he opened the back door and reached for the straps securing his son in the car seat. Complete and utter adoration welled in his heart as he lifted Evan Christopher from the seat and cradled him in the crook of his arm. "He's absolutely perfect," Keith murmured.

"He's an absolute pistol," Sara said with a smile, running her hand over the spirals of red hair on Evan's head. "Twelve hours of labor. Then he couldn't make an ordinary entrance."

Evan had arrived squalling and indignant at 2:00 a.m. three days ago, showing every sign of being a scrapper right from the start. Keith pressed a kiss to Sara's forehead. "He's got his mother's fighting spirit."

"I'd say his dad's stubbornness," Sara said with a laugh, then spotted the VW bug parked beside the house. "Ashley's here already."

Keith grabbed the diaper bag from the seat. "I left the key under the mat for her."

Ashley came out on the front porch, the door open for Sara. She toned down her usually ebullient hug in consideration for Sara's stitches, then escorted her sister to the living room sofa.

His son still snuggled in his arm, Keith watched the two sisters side by side on the sofa. Ashley was like a smaller version of her sister, shorter, slimmer, her hair a more well-behaved strawberry-blond, unlike the wild auburn curls on Sara's head. Knowing how much his wife loved having her sister around, he'd been glad to hear Ashley would be looking for a job close to Hart Valley after her June graduation from Berkeley next month.

Ashley started toward him, arms outstretched. "Okay, give, brother-in-law."

As he handed Evan over to Ashley, he caught Sara's gaze and smiled. Emotion surged inside him at the precious gifts he'd been given—his wife, his son.

In the ten months since their marriage, Keith never let

a day pass without telling his wife how much he loved her. He'd learned life could stop and turn on a dime, and although he wouldn't obsess over the pain of the past, he was learning to savor each moment of the present. Sara had taught him about forgiveness, about love. Every day with her filled him with gratitude.

When he saw Sara's wide yawn, he went to her and held out his hand. "You need a nap."

She rose slowly from the sofa. "I fed him at the hospital," she told Ashley as they passed her. "Wake me when he's hungry."

His arm around her shoulders, Keith walked with Sara down the hallway to their bedroom. Once he had her tucked into bed, he kissed her, letting his mouth linger against hers.

She sighed. "I'm going to be out of commission for two months."

He stroked her cheek. "I look forward to your return to duty."

Her eyes at half-mast, she gazed up at him. "I love you, Keith."

"And I love you, sweetheart." He leaned close, whispering in her ear. "Thank you for my miracle."

* * * * *

Watch for Ashley's story,
HER BABY'S HERO, by Karen Sandler,
coming to you in April, 2006—
from Silhouette Special Edition!

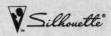

SPECIAL EDITION™

THE ROAD TO REUNION
by Gina Wilkins

Kyle Reeves vowed to keep a safe distance
from his longtime crush, but seeing
Molly Walker at his doorstep only intensified
the desire for her that he'd kept bottled up
for years. When Molly got injured, Kyle had
no choice but to return to the only home
he'd ever known and confront the woman
who stole his heart.

HOME AT LAST...

Available February 2006

Where love comes alive™

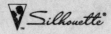
Silhouette®

SPECIAL EDITION™

HUSBANDS AND OTHER STRANGERS

by

Marie Ferrarella

A boating accident left Gayle Elliott Conway with amnesia and no recollection of the handsome man who came to her rescue…her husband. Convinced there was more to the story, Taylor Conway set out for answers and a way back into the heart of the woman he loved.

Available February 2006

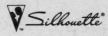

SPECIAL EDITION™

IT RUNS IN THE FAMILY

The second book in *USA TODAY* bestselling
author Patricia Kay's lighthearted miniseries

Callie's Corner Café:
It's where good friends meet…

Zoe Madison's fling with a rock star was ancient
history, until her daughter, Emma, flew to L.A.
to meet the star…and discovered he was her
father! Could Zoe protect Emma from her
newfound dad's empty Hollywood promises?
Maybe, with the help of a special man.…

Available February 2006

You can also catch up with the
Callie's Corner Café gang in

A PERFECT LIFE, January 2006
SHE'S THE ONE, March 2006

Where love comes alive™

If you enjoyed what you just read,
then we've got an offer you can't resist!

Take 2 bestselling
love stories FREE!
Plus get a FREE surprise gift!

Clip this page and mail it to Silhouette Reader Service™

IN U.S.A.
3010 Walden Ave.
P.O. Box 1867
Buffalo, N.Y. 14240-1867

IN CANADA
P.O. Box 609
Fort Erie, Ontario
L2A 5X3

YES! Please send me 2 free Silhouette Special Edition® novels and my free surprise gift. After receiving them, if I don't wish to receive anymore, I can return the shipping statement marked cancel. If I don't cancel, I will receive 6 brand-new novels every month, before they're available in stores! In the U.S.A., bill me at the bargain price of $4.24 plus 25¢ shipping and handling per book and applicable sales tax, if any*. In Canada, bill me at the bargain price of $4.99 plus 25¢ shipping and handling per book and applicable taxes**. That's the complete price and a savings of at least 10% off the cover prices—what a great deal! I understand that accepting the 2 free books and gift places me under no obligation ever to buy any books. I can always return a shipment and cancel at any time. Even if I never buy another book from Silhouette, the 2 free books and gift are mine to keep forever.

235 SDN DZ9D
335 SDN DZ9E

Name	(PLEASE PRINT)	
Address	Apt.#	
City	State/Prov.	Zip/Postal Code

Not valid to current Silhouette Special Edition® subscribers.

Want to try two free books from another series?
Call 1-800-873-8635 or visit www.morefreebooks.com.

* Terms and prices subject to change without notice. Sales tax applicable in N.Y.
** Canadian residents will be charged applicable provincial taxes and GST.
   All orders subject to approval. Offer limited to one per household.
   ® are registered trademarks owned and used by the trademark owner and or its licensee.

SPED04R   ©2004 Harlequin Enterprises Limited

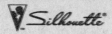

SPECIAL EDITION™

presents a new continuity

FAMILY BUSINESS:

Bound by fate, a shattered family renews their ties—and finds a legacy of love.

Don't miss a single exciting title
from *Family Business:*

PRODIGAL SON
by Susan Mallery, January 2006

THE BOSS AND MISS BAXTER
by Wendy Warren, February 2006

THE BABY DEAL
by Victoria Pade, March 2006

FALLING FOR THE BOSS
by Elizabeth Harbison, April 2006

HER BEST-KEPT SECRET
by Brenda Harlen, May 2006

MERGERS & MATRIMONY
by Allison Leigh, June 2006

Where love comes alive™

Three friends, two exes and a plan to get payback.

The Payback Club
by Rexanne Becnel
USA TODAY BESTSELLING AUTHOR

Available January 2006
TheNextNovel.com

COMING NEXT MONTH

SPECIAL EDITION